DARREN FAHY

The Dream Equation

Copyright © 2024 by Darren Fahy

All rights reserved. No part of this publication may be reproduced, stored or transmitted in any form or by any means, electronic, mechanical, photocopying, recording, scanning, or otherwise without written permission from the publisher. It is illegal to copy this book, post it to a website, or distribute it by any other means without permission.

First edition

This book was professionally typeset on Reedsy.
Find out more at reedsy.com

To Joe,

For always being there with a helping hand, even in the toughest moments. Your friendship has been a guiding light, a steady presence, and a source of inspiration. Thank you for being a constant reminder of what it means to care, to support, and to believe.

This story, like so much in life, is better because of you.

Contents

Chapter 1 - The Dream — 1
Chapter 2 - First Attempts — 5
Chapter 3 - Patterns in the Data — 8
Chapter 4 - A Breakthrough — 12
Chapter 5 - Shadows of Doubt — 16
Chapter 6 - Initial Experiments — 20
Chapter 7 - Attracting Attention — 24
Chapter 8 - Ethical Dilemmas — 28
Chapter 9 - The Unexpected Ally — 32
Chapter 10 – Shadows of the Past — 36
Chapter 11 - Pushing the Limits — 39
Chapter 12 - The Observation — 44
Chapter 13 – The Insider — 49
Chapter 14 - The Spy — 53
Chapter 15 - The Ultimatum — 58
Chapter 16 – The Past That Warns — 62
Chapter 17 - The Breakthrough — 65
Chapter 18 – A Glimpse Beyond — 70
Chapter 19 - The Fracture — 74
Chapter 20 - The Quiet Before the Storm — 79
Chapter 21 - The Confrontation — 85
Chapter 22 - The Escape — 90
Chapter 23 – Atlas Strikes — 95
Chapter 24 - The Formula's True Potential — 100
Chapter 25 - The Cost of Knowledge — 105
Chapter 26 - Sacrifice — 110

Chapter 27 - Reflection	115
Chapter 28 - The Legacy	119
About the Author	122

Chapter 1 - The Dream

The dream began like a burst of static, a flicker of light against a vast, endless void. Shapes swirled in Isaac's vision—numbers and symbols, their edges glowing faintly as they moved in impossible patterns. He couldn't make sense of them, yet he felt a strange familiarity, like recalling a song from his childhood he couldn't quite name. The symbols pulsed, shifting faster, rearranging themselves in fractals and waves, each movement creating a deep hum that resonated in his chest.

He reached out in the dream, his fingers brushing against the glowing patterns. The hum grew louder.

Then he woke, gasping for air.

Isaac bolted upright in his bed, his chest heaving. His dorm room was bathed in faint moonlight, the quiet hum of his desk fan the only sound breaking the silence. Sweat clung to his skin, and his hands trembled as he rubbed his face. For a moment, he stared at the ceiling, willing his racing heart to calm.

But the symbols were still there.

They danced in his mind's eye, vivid and clear, refusing to fade like most dreams. Without thinking, Isaac reached for the notebook on his nightstand. Flipping it open, he grabbed a pen and began to write.

His hand moved in a frenzy, driven by an urgency he didn't fully understand. Numbers, symbols, and lines poured onto the page, jagged and uneven but unmistakable in their clarity. He wasn't thinking about what he was writing—he simply had to get it out before it disappeared.

The pen slipped from his fingers as he finished, his hand cramping from the effort. He sat back against his pillow, staring at the notebook. The page was a chaotic web of equations and symbols, some of which he recognized from advanced calculus, while others were completely alien.

A chill ran down his spine.

It didn't feel like something he'd created. It felt like something he'd been given.

*　*　*

The next morning, sunlight streamed through the blinds, painting golden slats across the cluttered desk. Isaac sat hunched over his notebook, his breakfast forgotten on the windowsill. He traced the lines of the equations with his finger, his mind racing to make sense of them.

The formulas had an elegance to them, a strange beauty that drew him in. Certain symbols reminded him of concepts from his quantum mechanics class, while others seemed to hint at patterns in nature—the spirals of galaxies, the veins of leaves. But none of it fit together.

His phone buzzed, pulling him from his thoughts.

Harry: *Breakfast? Same spot?*

Isaac smiled faintly. Trust Harry to keep things simple. Tossing the notebook into his bag, he grabbed his coat and headed out.

*　*　*

The cafeteria buzzed with its usual morning chaos. Students crowded around tables, balancing trays piled with pancakes and coffee while laughing about last night's assignments or groaning about upcoming exams.

Isaac spotted Harry at their usual table by the window, hunched over his laptop with a half-eaten bagel in one hand. His dark hair was perpetually

CHAPTER 1 - THE DREAM

disheveled, and his jacket bore a coffee stain that Isaac was sure had been there for weeks.

"You're late," Harry said without looking up as Isaac slid into the seat across from him.

"And you're predictable," Isaac countered, setting his bag on the floor. He pulled out the notebook and placed it on the table. "Take a look at this."

Harry raised an eyebrow, finally closing his laptop. "What, another one of your sleep-deprived ideas?"

"Just look," Isaac said, sliding the notebook toward him.

Harry flipped it open, his expression shifting from mild curiosity to confusion. He leaned in closer, scanning the equations. "What the hell is this? Did you dream up calculus last night?"

"Something like that," Isaac said, leaning forward. "I woke up and just… wrote it all down. I don't even know what half of it means, but it doesn't feel random. There's a structure to it."

Harry flipped another page, frowning. "A structure? Isaac, half of this looks like gibberish. You've got squiggles next to actual math symbols."

"It's not gibberish," Isaac insisted. "I've been looking at it all morning. Some of it matches things I've seen in quantum mechanics, but other parts… it's like they're from another language."

Harry studied him for a long moment, then leaned back in his chair with a smirk. "Alright, genius. What's the plan? Decode the meaning of life? Build a time machine? Blow up the dorm?"

Isaac rolled his eyes but couldn't suppress a small smile. "I don't know yet. I just have a feeling this matters. I can't explain it, but I need to figure it out."

"Well," Harry said, picking up his bagel, "let me know when you crack it. Until then, try not to get yourself institutionalized. Dream math is a slippery slope."

* * *

That night, Isaac sat at his desk, his dorm room dimly lit by the glow of his laptop. The formula lay open beside him, its symbols staring back at him like a challenge. His fingers hovered over the keyboard, hesitating before typing out another equation.

The numbers on the screen blurred as his mind darted between possibilities. He tried to connect the fragments to existing theories—geometry, string theory, even chaos math—but every attempt felt like jamming mismatched puzzle pieces together.

Hours passed, the world outside his window fading into silence. His phone buzzed, breaking the stillness.

Harry: Still alive?

Isaac: Barely. Making progress, I think.

Harry: Don't die over it. Formula's not worth frying your brain.

Isaac smiled faintly, setting the phone aside. He glanced back at the notebook, his resolve hardening.

The formula wasn't just a dream. It wasn't just math. It was something more.

And Isaac wasn't about to let it slip through his fingers.

Chapter 2 - First Attempts

The sound of typing filled Isaac's dorm room, accompanied by the faint hum of his desk lamp. Isaac sat cross-legged on his chair, his notebook propped open beside his laptop. His eyes darted between the two as he transferred the dream formula into a spreadsheet. The glow of the screen reflected off his glasses, highlighting the exhaustion etched into his face.

The knock on his door startled him.

"Still alive in there, Einstein?" Harry's voice called from the hallway.

Isaac grinned despite himself and got up to let him in. Harry strolled inside, holding two cups of coffee. He wore his usual hoodie and sneakers, his backpack slung casually over one shoulder.

"Brought reinforcements," Harry said, handing Isaac a cup. "Thought you might need it."

"Thanks," Isaac replied, taking a sip. The coffee was lukewarm and overly sweet, but he appreciated the gesture.

Harry glanced around the room, taking in the stacks of books, scattered papers, and the half-empty energy drink cans on Isaac's desk. "Wow. You've really gone full mad scientist, haven't you?"

Isaac smirked, but his focus returned to the screen. "Take a look at this," he said, gesturing to his laptop.

Harry pulled up a chair and leaned in. "Alright, let's see what's keeping you from being a functional human being."

The screen displayed rows of equations, some straightforward, others twisting into unfamiliar territory. Harry squinted at them, his expression shifting from mild curiosity to confusion.

"Okay, I'm not gonna lie," Harry said after a moment. "This looks like the kind of math that gets people expelled for trying to summon demons."

Isaac chuckled. "It's not that bad. Look here." He pointed to one of the rows. "This part matches something I've seen in quantum mechanics—describes particle behavior. But this..." He highlighted another section. "This doesn't follow any rules I know. It's like it's building on the concept but also rewriting it."

Harry leaned back in his chair, rubbing his chin. "So, let me get this straight. You dreamed this up, wrote it down, and now it's rewriting physics as we know it?"

Isaac shrugged. "Maybe. Or maybe it's nothing. But I can't stop thinking about it, Harry. It's like it's waiting for me to figure it out."

Harry tilted his head, studying Isaac. "You know, most people would have just chalked this up to a weird dream and moved on with their lives. You're really going all in on this, huh?"

Isaac sighed, his gaze drifting to the notebook. "I don't know how to explain it. It doesn't feel random. It feels... deliberate. Like I didn't create it—I just found it."

Harry stared at him for a moment, then shook his head with a grin. "You're lucky I don't have a social life, or I wouldn't be putting up with this level of nerd obsession."

Isaac smirked. "You love it."

Harry stood, grabbing a stack of Isaac's papers and flipping through them. "Alright, genius. Let's humor this. If this formula's as groundbreaking as you think, what's the next step?"

Isaac hesitated, biting his lip. "I've been running some tests, trying to match the patterns to known equations, but... I'm stuck. There's something I'm missing."

Harry's grin widened. "That's where I come in. Hand me that notebook."

Isaac handed it over, watching as Harry scanned the pages. Unlike Isaac's meticulous focus, Harry's approach was more intuitive—quick, broad strokes that picked out key elements.

"This part here," Harry said, pointing to a line. "You're treating it like a

CHAPTER 2 - FIRST ATTEMPTS

standalone equation, but what if it's not? What if it's a key to something bigger—like a cipher?"

Isaac frowned, leaning over to see where Harry was pointing. "A cipher? You think the whole formula is some kind of code?"

"Why not?" Harry said with a shrug. "It would explain why it doesn't fit into anything you've studied. It's not just solving problems—it's unlocking them."

Isaac sat back, considering the idea. It was a perspective he hadn't thought of, and it sparked something in his mind. "That... actually makes sense. If I isolate the constants and treat them like variables..."

He grabbed his laptop, typing furiously. Harry leaned back in his chair, sipping his coffee with a satisfied smirk.

* * *

Hours later, the room was a chaotic mess of papers, books, and empty coffee cups. Isaac and Harry worked side by side, bouncing ideas off each other as they dissected the formula.

Every now and then, one of them would have a breakthrough—a connection between two fragments, a new way of interpreting a symbol. But just as often, they hit dead ends, leading to groans of frustration.

"It's like trying to decode an alien language," Harry muttered, running a hand through his hair.

"Maybe it is," Isaac replied, only half-joking.

Finally, as the first rays of dawn crept through the blinds, they stepped back from the desk. The notebook was filled with annotations, and the laptop screen displayed a partial framework of the formula—a skeleton waiting to be fleshed out.

Harry raised his coffee cup in a toast. "To dream math."

Isaac chuckled, clinking his mug against Harry's. "And to figuring out what the hell it is."

Chapter 3 - Patterns in the Data

The library at Ridley Institute was nearly deserted, its towering shelves of books casting long, dark shadows under the dim glow of overhead lights. Isaac sat in his usual spot in the far corner, surrounded by open textbooks, loose papers, and his ever-present notebook. His laptop hummed softly, its screen a patchwork of graphs, equations, and hastily scribbled notes.

He leaned back in his chair, rubbing his temples. Hours had passed, but the formula refused to reveal its secrets. Every connection he thought he'd uncovered unraveled into something more complex. The data didn't just resist explanation—it seemed to change as he studied it.

Across the table, Harry was sprawled in his chair, one sneakered foot resting on the corner of the desk. He chewed absentmindedly on the end of a pen, his eyes darting between Isaac's laptop and the notebook in his lap.

"You look like you're about to set this place on fire," Harry said, breaking the silence.

Isaac let out a sharp breath, running a hand through his hair. "It's maddening. I know there's something here, but it's like… it's alive. Every time I think I'm onto something, it shifts."

Harry straightened, leaning forward. "Alright, genius, let's take a step back. Walk me through what you're seeing."

Isaac gestured to the screen. "This part here—it's like a lattice. A structure, but it's dynamic. It changes based on the inputs. I've never seen anything like it."

Harry squinted at the monitor, his brow furrowing. "You're saying it reacts to what you feed it? Like, it adapts?"

CHAPTER 3 - PATTERNS IN THE DATA

"Exactly," Isaac said, his voice quickening with excitement. "It's not just solving equations—it's creating them. It's like it's building something, but I don't know what."

Harry leaned back again, crossing his arms. "That's not normal, right? Math isn't supposed to do that."

Isaac shook his head, his eyes still fixed on the screen. "No. It's not."

*　*　*

They worked in silence for a while, the only sounds the occasional rustle of papers and the faint hum of the library's air conditioning. Isaac entered another set of variables, his fingers flying over the keyboard. The graphs on the screen shifted again, forming a series of intricate fractals that pulsed faintly, almost as if they were alive.

Harry watched with a mix of awe and unease. "It's beautiful, I'll give you that. But it's also… unsettling."

Isaac didn't respond. His attention was fixed on the data, his mind racing. The patterns weren't random—they couldn't be. There was a rhythm to them, a logic he couldn't quite grasp.

"Wait," he said suddenly, his voice cutting through the quiet.

Harry leaned forward. "What?"

Isaac pointed to the screen. "Look at this."

Harry frowned, following Isaac's gaze. On the second monitor, a data stream scrolled rapidly, numbers and symbols flashing too quickly to follow. But one set of figures stood out—a repeating sequence buried within the chaos.

"That wasn't there before," Isaac said, his voice barely a whisper.

"What does it mean?" Harry asked, his tone cautious.

Isaac shook his head. "I don't know. But it's deliberate. It has to be."

Harry tapped the edge of the desk, his expression thoughtful. "So, it's not just adapting—it's leaving breadcrumbs. Like it wants you to follow it."

THE DREAM EQUATION

Isaac glanced at him, a chill running down his spine. "You think it's trying to communicate?"

Harry shrugged, though his unease was clear. "I don't know what to think. But if this thing is more than just numbers..." He trailed off, letting the implication hang in the air.

* * *

As the hours dragged on, the patterns became clearer, though no less mysterious. Isaac worked tirelessly, isolating fragments of the formula and testing their behavior. Each piece seemed to hold a unique property, like notes in a symphony. Together, they formed something far greater than the sum of their parts.

Harry, meanwhile, began sketching connections in the notebook, linking symbols with lines and arrows. His approach was less methodical than Isaac's, but it yielded surprising insights.

"Look at this," he said, sliding the notebook across the table. "This part here—it mirrors something you've got on the screen. See?"

Isaac frowned, comparing the pages. Harry was right. The pattern Harry had traced matched one of the fractals on the monitor, though it was rotated and slightly distorted.

"It's the same," Isaac said, his voice tinged with awe. "But how did you—"

"Gut instinct," Harry said with a smirk. "Sometimes your brain needs a break from all the fancy math."

Isaac chuckled softly, though the discovery only deepened the mystery. If the formula was leaving patterns for them to find, what else might it reveal?

* * *

CHAPTER 3 - PATTERNS IN THE DATA

By the time the library began to fill with the morning's first visitors, Isaac and Harry were both running on fumes. Isaac saved his progress and shut down the laptop, while Harry stretched and let out a groan.

"You know," Harry said, gathering his things, "if this doesn't lead to a Nobel Prize, I'm suing you for wasting my time."

Isaac laughed, though his thoughts were elsewhere. The formula had given them more questions than answers, and he couldn't shake the feeling that they were only scratching the surface.

As they left the library, the sunlight felt harsh after hours in the dim interior. Isaac glanced at Harry, who was already rifling through his phone.

"You don't think this is just some... coincidence, do you?" Isaac asked.

Harry glanced up, his expression serious. "I don't believe in coincidences. But I do believe we're playing with something we don't fully understand. So let's be careful, yeah?"

Isaac nodded, though his mind was already racing ahead. Whatever the formula was, it wasn't just math.

And it wasn't done with them yet.

Chapter 4 - A Breakthrough

The Ridley Institute's engineering lab was a world away from the dim quiet of the library. The air was alive with the faint buzz of machines, the hum of high-powered computers processing massive data loads. Isaac and Harry had commandeered a workstation in the back corner, where Isaac's laptop was now tethered to a sleek custom-built system. Rows of monitors displayed the results of their latest tests: spiraling graphs, data streams, and glowing simulations that seemed to defy logic.

Harry leaned against the desk, arms crossed, watching as Isaac typed furiously. "I still don't get why we need all this firepower. I thought dream math didn't need a supercomputer."

Isaac glanced up briefly, his face illuminated by the glow of the monitors. "It's not just numbers, Harry. It's a system. The formula reacts to inputs—it adapts. The more data we feed it, the more it evolves. My laptop couldn't keep up."

Harry raised an eyebrow. "So, basically, you're saying we're building Frankenstein's monster out of math."

Isaac smirked. "Not quite. But I get the metaphor."

* * *

Isaac ran the next set of variables, his heart pounding as the system processed the inputs. On the main monitor, the screen flickered before resolving into a

CHAPTER 4 - A BREAKTHROUGH

three-dimensional lattice, its edges glowing faintly. The structure shifted in real time, morphing as the variables were adjusted.

"Whoa," Harry muttered, leaning closer. "That's... weirdly beautiful."

"It's a neural lattice," Isaac explained, his voice tinged with excitement. "The formula isn't just generating results—it's building a framework. A system that can learn."

Harry blinked, his expression a mix of awe and unease. "A system that can learn? Isaac, you realize what you're saying, right? This isn't just math anymore. It's something else."

Isaac hesitated, his gaze fixed on the lattice. He knew Harry was right, but he couldn't stop. The formula had taken on a life of its own, and it was pulling him deeper with every step.

"I know," Isaac said softly. "But don't you see the potential? If we understand how this works, we could change everything. Physics, computation, even biology—this formula could rewrite the rules of reality."

Harry ran a hand through his hair, his unease growing. "And what if it rewrites more than we bargained for? What if it's rewriting us?"

* * *

Hours later, the lab was silent except for the faint whir of the machines. Isaac had isolated a fragment of the formula, feeding it into a simulation designed to test its behavior under different conditions. On the monitor, the lattice pulsed faintly, shifting in ways that seemed almost... purposeful.

Harry watched from a safe distance, arms crossed. "So, let's talk about the elephant in the room. You're saying this thing can learn. What happens if it learns too much?"

Isaac sighed, leaning back in his chair. "It's not AI, Harry. It's just a framework. A tool."

"A tool that's starting to look an awful lot like it's alive," Harry countered. "Look, I'm not saying we stop. But we need to think about where this is going.

What happens if this thing falls into the wrong hands?"

Isaac frowned. "What do you mean?"

Harry gestured vaguely at the monitors. "Atlas Corporation, for starters. Or anyone who wants to weaponize this. Hell, even the university might decide it's worth more than we are."

Isaac leaned forward, his expression serious. "That's why we're careful. We don't share this with anyone until we understand it."

Harry didn't look convinced. "That's a nice thought, but you're assuming we'll stay in control. What if we can't?"

* * *

As the night wore on, Isaac continued testing the formula, running simulations and analyzing the outputs. The results were staggering—predictions, optimizations, and even what appeared to be solutions to problems Isaac hadn't posed.

At one point, Harry interrupted him. "Look at this," he said, pointing to a section of code.

Isaac leaned over, his brow furrowing. The formula had introduced a new variable—something neither of them had input.

"It's modifying itself," Harry said, his voice low.

Isaac stared at the screen, his mind racing. "It's… evolving."

"Isaac," Harry said, his tone sharp. "Do you not see how dangerous this is? This isn't just about understanding the formula anymore. It's doing things we didn't ask it to do."

Isaac nodded slowly, the weight of Harry's words sinking in. "You're right. We need to be careful."

* * *

CHAPTER 4 - A BREAKTHROUGH

Later that night, as they packed up the lab, Harry broached the topic again. "You know, this thing is going to raise some serious ethical questions."

Isaac glanced at him. "Like what?"

"Like whether we should even be doing this," Harry said. "What happens if this formula falls into the wrong hands? Or if it gets out of control?"

Isaac sighed. "I get it, Harry. But if we stop now, we'll never know what it's capable of. And what if it could change the world for the better?"

Harry shook his head. "Or destroy it. You're looking at this like a scientist, Isaac. But maybe you should start looking at it like a human being."

The words stung, but Isaac knew Harry wasn't wrong.

* * *

That night, back in his dorm, Isaac couldn't sleep. The formula filled his thoughts, its shifting patterns and infinite potential pulling him deeper. He opened his laptop and began researching ethical frameworks for scientific discovery, scrolling through articles on unintended consequences and the risks of unchecked innovation.

One quote stood out to him: *"Just because we can, doesn't mean we should."*

Isaac closed the laptop, staring at the notebook on his desk. The formula wasn't just a discovery—it was a responsibility.

And the weight of that responsibility was starting to feel like more than he could carry.

Chapter 5 - Shadows of Doubt

The dream was different this time.

Isaac stood in a vast, featureless void, its emptiness stretching into infinity. Suspended before him was the formula, its symbols glowing faintly, their edges rippling like heat waves. The symbols shifted constantly, forming shapes that defied comprehension—spirals, lattices, and impossible geometric constructs.

Then the presence returned.

It was everywhere and nowhere at once, vast and unyielding. Isaac felt it pressing down on him, heavy and suffocating, though it wasn't hostile. It simply was. A cold awareness that observed him as he reached out toward the formula.

His fingers brushed against the glowing symbols, and they pulsed under his touch. A deep hum vibrated through the void, rising in intensity until it became a roar.

"Why me?" Isaac whispered, his voice swallowed by the noise.

The formula flared blindingly bright, and then everything shattered into darkness.

Isaac woke with a start, gasping for air.

* * *

The notebook lay open on his desk, its pages filled with the strange, tangled

CHAPTER 5 - SHADOWS OF DOUBT

fragments of the formula. Isaac sat at the edge of his bed, staring at the symbols as his pulse slowly steadied.

This wasn't just math anymore. It was something else.

His phone buzzed on the nightstand, startling him. He grabbed it, squinting at the screen.

Harry: *Coffee. Now.*

Isaac sighed, running a hand through his hair. Leave it to Harry to ground him, even when everything else felt like it was spinning out of control.

* * *

The campus coffee shop was busy, but Isaac spotted Harry immediately. He was sitting at their usual corner table, laptop open, two steaming mugs in front of him.

"You look like hell," Harry said as Isaac slid into the seat across from him.

"Feel like it too," Isaac muttered, taking a sip of his coffee.

Harry leaned back, watching him carefully. "Let me guess. More dreams?"

Isaac nodded, his fingers tightening around the mug. "It's not just dreams anymore, Harry. It feels... real. Like the formula is trying to tell me something."

"Tell you what? That you're losing your mind?" Harry said, though his tone lacked its usual teasing edge.

Isaac hesitated. "I don't know. But it's not random. I feel like it's pulling me toward something—something big."

Harry frowned, his expression darkening. "Big doesn't mean good, Isaac. You've got to start thinking about the risks here. We don't know what this thing is—or what it's capable of."

* * *

THE DREAM EQUATION

Later that evening, Isaac sat alone in the library, the soft glow of his laptop screen the only light in the quiet space. He'd tried to distract himself with coursework, but his thoughts kept circling back to the formula.

He opened a new document, typing out everything he could remember from the dream. The symbols, the hum, the crushing presence—it all spilled onto the page, fragmented and messy.

As he worked, an uncomfortable question surfaced in his mind.

What if Harry was right? What if the formula wasn't just a discovery, but a danger?

Isaac leaned back in his chair, staring at the screen. The formula had already begun to take over his life. He was skipping lectures, neglecting assignments, and barely sleeping. His obsession was becoming a weight he couldn't ignore.

But every time he thought about walking away, the pull grew stronger.

* * *

The knock on his door came late that night, sharp and insistent. Isaac opened it to find Harry standing there, his face unusually serious.

"We need to talk," Harry said, stepping inside without waiting for an invitation.

Isaac frowned. "About what?"

"About Atlas," Harry said, dropping a folder onto the desk.

Isaac's stomach tightened. "What about them?"

Harry gestured to the folder. "They've been poking around. I overheard one of the lab assistants talking about some consultant visiting campus last week. Guess who they're working for?"

Isaac opened the folder, skimming the printed emails and notes inside. His heart sank.

Atlas Corporation wasn't just watching them—they were circling.

"You know what they'll do if they get their hands on this, right?" Harry said, his voice low. "They'll take it. Own it. Turn it into something we can't

CHAPTER 5 - SHADOWS OF DOUBT

control."

Isaac sat down heavily, the weight of the folder in his hands. "Why would they care about my research? It's not even finished."

Harry shook his head. "Doesn't matter. They've got people who can sniff out potential like bloodhounds. And you're bleeding potential, Isaac."

* * *

That night, Isaac couldn't sleep. The weight of Harry's words pressed down on him like a physical force. He stared at the notebook on his desk, its symbols glowing faintly under the moonlight.

What was the formula, really?

For weeks, he'd thought of it as a discovery—something extraordinary that could change the world. But now, he wasn't so sure.

If Atlas got their hands on it, they'd twist it into something unrecognizable. A weapon, maybe. Or a tool for control.

And then there was the dream. The presence. The feeling that the formula wasn't just math, but something alive.

Isaac stood, crossing the room to pick up the notebook. He flipped through the pages slowly, his fingers tracing the lines of the equations.

"Just because I can," he whispered to himself, "doesn't mean I should."

But even as he said the words, he knew he couldn't stop. The formula had already consumed him, and he wasn't sure if he'd ever get free.

Chapter 6 - Initial Experiments

The engineering lab hummed with quiet energy, its rows of sleek monitors and humming machinery casting faint shadows in the dim light. Isaac sat at the central workstation, his laptop connected to the lab's high-performance computer. Harry stood behind him, arms crossed, watching as Isaac keyed in the final variables.

"Alright," Isaac said, leaning back in his chair. "That should do it."

Harry didn't move, his gaze fixed on the screen. "You're sure about this?"

Isaac looked up at him, his face illuminated by the glow of the monitor. "No. But we've been theorizing for weeks. We need to see what it can do."

Harry exhaled sharply, running a hand through his hair. "Fine. Just promise me we're not about to accidentally summon some kind of cyber-demon."

Isaac smirked faintly, though his hands trembled as they hovered over the keyboard. "No demons. Just math." He hit the enter key.

The machines whirred to life, their fans spinning up as the system processed the inputs. Lines of code scrolled rapidly across the screen, while graphs and data visualizations began to form on the monitors.

At first, everything seemed normal. The system processed the formula like any other complex calculation. But then, something changed.

The graphs shifted, their lines breaking apart and reforming into intricate fractals. On the second monitor, a glowing lattice structure appeared, pulsing faintly as it evolved in real time.

Harry leaned forward, his brow furrowing. "That's... not normal."

"It's adapting," Isaac whispered, his eyes wide. "It's building something—a framework."

CHAPTER 6 - INITIAL EXPERIMENTS

Harry shook his head, his unease growing. "Adapting to what? You didn't program this."

"No," Isaac said, his voice filled with awe. "But it's responding to the inputs. It's optimizing itself."

* * *

The lattice on the screen grew more intricate with each passing second, its edges glowing as it shifted and pulsed. Isaac's heart raced as he watched, his mind struggling to keep up with what he was seeing.

"This isn't just a formula anymore," Harry said, breaking the silence. "It's a system. A system that's learning."

Isaac didn't respond. He was too engrossed in the lattice, his thoughts racing. The formula wasn't just solving equations—it was creating them. It was generating patterns that felt almost… alive.

Harry stepped back, crossing his arms. "Okay, I'm officially freaked out. What happens if it keeps going? Do we even know where this is headed?"

Isaac shook his head. "No. But that's the point. This is uncharted territory, Harry. We're discovering something completely new."

"Or something completely dangerous," Harry muttered.

* * *

Hours passed as they ran test after test, each yielding results more complex and baffling than the last. The lattice structure continued to evolve, its patterns growing more intricate and interconnected. At one point, the system introduced a new variable—something neither Isaac nor Harry had input.

"What the hell is that?" Harry asked, pointing to the screen.

Isaac frowned, his fingers flying over the keyboard as he pulled up the data.

THE DREAM EQUATION

"It's... a modification. The system is rewriting part of the formula."

Harry stared at him. "It's rewriting itself? Isaac, that's not normal. That's not even close to normal."

Isaac leaned back, his mind spinning. "It's evolving. It's responding to the environment and creating new outputs. Harry, this could be—"

"A disaster waiting to happen," Harry interrupted. He gestured to the screen, his voice rising. "You're looking at this like a scientist, but maybe you should start looking at it like a human being. What happens if this thing gets out of control?"

Isaac opened his mouth to respond, but no words came.

* * *

As the simulation continued, Isaac couldn't shake the growing weight in his chest. The formula was incredible—beyond anything he'd ever imagined. But Harry's words lingered in his mind.

He thought of Atlas Corporation. If they got their hands on this...

Isaac shuddered at the thought. He knew what Atlas was capable of. They wouldn't see the formula as a discovery—they'd see it as a weapon.

"We need to be careful," Isaac said finally, his voice quiet.

Harry raised an eyebrow. "Now you're catching on."

* * *

That night, back in his dorm, Isaac sat at his desk, staring at the notebook. The formula's symbols glowed faintly under the desk lamp, their patterns still vivid in his mind.

He opened his laptop and began typing, recording everything they'd observed during the experiments. The lattice, the self-modification, the

CHAPTER 6 - INITIAL EXPERIMENTS

patterns that felt too deliberate to be random.

As he worked, he came across a research paper he'd saved weeks ago. It explored the idea of emergent intelligence—how sufficiently complex systems could begin to exhibit behaviors that mimicked thought.

Isaac read the abstract again, his chest tightening.

What if the formula wasn't just math? What if it was something more?

His phone buzzed, breaking his concentration.

Harry: *Go to sleep. Seriously. The formula will still be there tomorrow.*

Isaac smiled faintly, but he didn't close his laptop. He couldn't stop now—not when he was so close.

Whatever the formula was, it wasn't just a discovery. It was a doorway.

And Isaac had no choice but to step through.

Chapter 7 - Attracting Attention

The Ridley Institute's campus was quiet that morning, blanketed by a fog that blurred the edges of the old brick buildings. Isaac walked briskly toward the physics building, clutching his bag tightly against his side. The faint buzz of his phone in his pocket interrupted his thoughts, and he pulled it out, expecting another message from Harry.

But it wasn't Harry. It was an email.

Isaac's steps slowed as he read the subject line: **"Collaboration Opportunity."** The sender's name made his stomach drop: **Atlas Corporation.**

He stopped in his tracks, the chill in the air suddenly feeling sharper. Atlas.

For a moment, he hesitated, his thumb hovering over the screen. He knew the reputation. Atlas Corporation wasn't just a tech powerhouse—it was an enigma, a shadow that loomed over every field of advanced research. They had pioneered breakthroughs in quantum computing, AI, and even energy systems that bordered on science fiction. But their history was littered with darker rumors.

Scientists who disappeared after working with them. Entire labs that went dark, their projects buried under layers of corporate secrecy. The whispers about Atlas weren't just tales—they were warnings.

Isaac swallowed hard and opened the email.

Dear Mr. Moreau,

We have recently become aware of your promising research and would like to discuss a potential partnership. Atlas Corporation prides itself on fostering innovation and providing unparalleled resources to visionary minds like yours. Should you wish to explore this opportunity further,

CHAPTER 7 - ATTRACTING ATTENTION

please respond to this email at your earliest convenience.

Isaac's heart pounded as he read the message again. It was polite, professional, and disturbingly vague. But the implications were clear. They knew.

* * *

By the time he reached the lab, Isaac felt a knot of anxiety twisting in his chest. Harry was already there, sitting cross-legged on the counter with a coffee in one hand and his phone in the other.

"Morning, Einstein," Harry said without looking up. "You look like you've seen a ghost."

Isaac dropped his bag onto the table, his movements jerky. "Atlas emailed me."

Harry froze, his coffee halfway to his mouth. Slowly, he set the cup down. "Atlas? As in the Atlas Corporation?"

Isaac nodded, pulling out his laptop and opening the email. Harry leaned over his shoulder, reading the message.

"'Aware of your promising research'? How the hell do they know what we're working on?" Harry demanded, his voice rising.

Isaac shook his head. "I don't know. But they're interested. And that scares me."

Harry stepped back, pacing the room. "Yeah, well, it should scare you. Do you know what they do, Isaac? Atlas doesn't collaborate—they consume. They fund you, they own you, and then they bury you. End of story."

Isaac's stomach churned as he watched Harry pace. "Maybe it's just a generic email. Maybe they don't actually know—"

"Don't kid yourself," Harry interrupted, his voice sharp. "Atlas doesn't send emails for no reason. If they're reaching out, it's because they want something. And you're it."

Isaac sighed, running a hand through his hair. "What do I do? I can't just ignore them."

"You absolutely can," Harry snapped. "You hit delete, and you lock this formula down so tight they can't sniff it out again."

* * *

Later that afternoon, as Isaac worked alone in the lab, the tension refused to leave him. The monitors glowed faintly, displaying the latest data from their experiments. The lattice was still evolving, its patterns shifting like the heartbeat of some unseen organism.

Isaac stared at it, his mind racing. Atlas didn't just want the formula—they wanted control. And if they got it, the implications were terrifying.

The sound of footsteps broke his thoughts. He looked up to see Dr. Patel standing in the doorway, her arms crossed.

"Isaac," she said, her tone carefully neutral. "Can we talk?"

Isaac nodded slowly. "Sure."

Dr. Patel stepped into the room, her gaze sweeping over the monitors. "You've been putting in a lot of hours here lately. Care to share what's been keeping you so busy?"

Isaac hesitated. "Just a project I've been working on. It's… complicated."

Dr. Patel raised an eyebrow. "Complicated enough to draw the attention of Atlas Corporation?"

Isaac's stomach dropped. "How do you know about that?"

She smiled faintly. "I have my sources. And I know how Atlas operates. Let me guess—they sent you a polite little email about a 'collaboration opportunity,' didn't they?"

Isaac nodded, unsure of what to say.

Dr. Patel sighed, leaning against the counter. "Atlas approached me once, years ago. I was fresh out of my postdoc program, eager to make a name for myself. They offered me funding—more money than I'd ever seen—and all they wanted was access to my research. It seemed like the opportunity of a lifetime."

"What happened?" Isaac asked, his voice quiet.

"They owned it," Dr. Patel said bluntly. "Every equation, every paper, every idea I had—it all became theirs. And when I realized what was happening and tried to back out, they shut everything down. My lab, my career, my work—it was all gone."

Isaac stared at her, the weight of her words sinking in. "Why are you telling me this?"

"Because I see where this is going," Dr. Patel said. "You're standing on the edge of something big, Isaac. And Atlas will do everything in their power to take it from you. You need to be careful."

Isaac nodded slowly, her warning echoing Harry's earlier words.

* * *

That night, Isaac sat in his dorm, staring at his laptop. The Atlas email was still open on the screen, its polite tone feeling more ominous with each passing hour.

He opened a new document and began typing, recording everything he'd learned about the company. Their history, their tactics, their reputation—it all painted a picture of a corporation willing to do whatever it took to stay ahead.

His phone buzzed, a message from Harry.

Harry: *Did you delete it yet?*

Isaac stared at the message for a long moment before typing back.

Isaac: *Not yet. But I'm going to.*

He closed the laptop, his chest heavy with the weight of the decision.

Atlas was circling, and he wasn't sure how long he could keep them at bay.

Chapter 8 - Ethical Dilemmas

The engineering lab felt colder than usual, the hum of the machines punctuated by Harry's pacing footsteps. Isaac sat at the workstation, staring at the glowing lattice on the monitor. Its pulsing patterns had become familiar over the past few weeks, but tonight they seemed more alive, more deliberate.

"This has to stop," Harry said abruptly, breaking the silence.

Isaac turned to look at him, frowning. "What are you talking about?"

Harry gestured at the monitor, his frustration evident. "This. The formula. The experiments. All of it. We're playing with something we don't understand, Isaac, and it's getting out of hand."

Isaac sighed, leaning back in his chair. "We've been over this. The formula is important, Harry. You've seen the results. This could change everything."

"Yeah, that's what scares me," Harry shot back. "Do you even hear yourself? You're so focused on what it could do that you're ignoring what it might already be doing."

Isaac frowned, his gaze drifting back to the monitor. "What do you mean?"

Harry stopped pacing, leaning against the desk. "I mean we're treating this thing like it's just math, but it's not. It's learning, Isaac. It's evolving. And you're acting like we can just keep poking at it without consequences."

* * *

For a long moment, neither of them spoke. The lattice on the screen shifted,

CHAPTER 8 - ETHICAL DILEMMAS

its edges glowing faintly as it reconfigured itself. Isaac watched it with a mixture of awe and unease.

"Look," Harry said, his voice softer now. "I get it. You're brilliant, and this formula is incredible. But brilliance doesn't mean you can ignore the risks. What happens if this thing gets out? What happens if Atlas gets their hands on it?"

Isaac's jaw tightened at the mention of Atlas. "They won't. I won't let them."

Harry scoffed. "You think you can stop them? You're a grad student, Isaac. They're a multi-billion-dollar corporation with resources you can't even imagine. If they want this, they'll take it."

Isaac didn't respond. He knew Harry was right, but he couldn't bring himself to admit it.

* * *

The tension lingered between them as they returned to their work. Harry sat at the opposite end of the lab, reviewing the notes they'd compiled, while Isaac ran another simulation.

Hours passed, the lab's hum the only sound breaking the silence.

"Got something," Harry said suddenly, his tone grim.

Isaac looked up as Harry walked over, holding the notebook. "This part here," Harry said, pointing to a section of the formula. "It's not just adapting—it's predicting. The outputs aren't random. They're responses to things we haven't even input yet."

Isaac frowned, taking the notebook from him. He studied the equations, his stomach twisting. Harry was right. The formula was extrapolating data from their inputs and generating solutions to problems they hadn't posed.

"It's anticipating us," Isaac murmured, his voice barely audible.

Harry crossed his arms. "Exactly. And if it's doing that now, what's it going to do next?"

THE DREAM EQUATION

* * *

The conversation weighed heavily on Isaac as he walked back to his dorm that night. The campus was quiet, the lamplight casting long shadows across the cobblestone paths.

As he reached his room, he found himself thinking about Dr. Patel. She'd warned him about Atlas, about the dangers of letting the formula fall into the wrong hands. But she'd also spoken about the responsibility that came with discovery—the ethical questions he hadn't allowed himself to face.

Isaac sat at his desk, staring at the notebook. The formula's symbols seemed to glow faintly in the dim light, their intricate patterns both beautiful and unsettling.

"Just because we can," he murmured to himself, "doesn't mean we should."

But even as he said the words, he knew he couldn't stop.

* * *

The next day, Isaac found Dr. Patel in her office, surrounded by stacks of books and papers. She looked up as he knocked, her expression shifting from surprise to concern.

"Isaac," she said. "What's going on?"

"I need your advice," he said, stepping inside and closing the door behind him.

Dr. Patel gestured for him to sit, folding her hands on the desk. "I'm listening."

Isaac hesitated, then pulled out the notebook and set it in front of her. "It's about the formula."

Her gaze sharpened as she opened the notebook, scanning the pages. She said nothing for a long moment, her expression unreadable.

"Isaac," she said finally, her tone careful, "you know what you're dealing

CHAPTER 8 - ETHICAL DILEMMAS

with here, don't you?"

"I thought I did," he admitted. "But now I'm not so sure."

Dr. Patel closed the notebook, leaning back in her chair. "This isn't just a discovery. It's a responsibility. And it's one you need to take seriously."

Isaac nodded slowly. "I know. But Harry's worried. He thinks we're in over our heads, and... maybe he's right. I don't know what to do."

Dr. Patel studied him for a moment, then said, "The question you need to ask yourself isn't whether you can keep going—it's whether you should. The formula is extraordinary, Isaac, but it's also dangerous. You have to consider the consequences."

"What do you mean?"

"I mean that Atlas isn't the only risk here," she said. "This formula—whatever it is—has the potential to reshape everything we know about the world. Physics, computation, even life itself. But that kind of power can't be controlled. Not entirely. And if you're not careful, it could destroy everything you're trying to protect."

* * *

That evening, Isaac met Harry in the library. The tension between them had softened, but the weight of their conversation still lingered.

"We need to make a decision," Harry said, leaning forward across the table. "Do we keep going, or do we shut this down?"

Isaac hesitated, glancing at the notebook. The formula's pull was stronger than ever, but so was his fear.

"I don't know," he said finally. "But I think we need to figure that out together."

Harry nodded, his expression serious. "Yeah. Together."

Chapter 9 - The Unexpected Ally

Isaac knocked on Dr. Patel's office door, the notebook clutched tightly in his hand. The hum of fluorescent lights buzzed faintly in the corridor, but the campus felt unusually quiet, as if the entire world was holding its breath.

"Come in," came Dr. Patel's voice.

He stepped inside, his stomach tightening as he saw her seated at her desk, surrounded by stacks of research papers and textbooks. A steaming cup of tea sat untouched beside her, the faint scent of chai filling the air. She looked up, her sharp eyes immediately zeroing in on the notebook he held.

"Isaac," she said, leaning back in her chair. "What brings you here?"

He hesitated, gripping the notebook like a lifeline. "I need to talk to you. About the formula."

Dr. Patel's expression shifted slightly, her curiosity evident. She gestured for him to sit, folding her hands on the desk. "Alright. I'm listening."

***

For the next twenty minutes, Isaac explained everything. He spoke about the dream that had started it all, the experiments he and Harry had run, and the formula's increasingly unpredictable behavior. He didn't hold back, describing the lattice's evolution and the eerie feeling that the formula was alive—anticipating them.

Dr. Patel listened in silence, her expression unreadable as he laid everything

CHAPTER 9 - THE UNEXPECTED ALLY

bare. When he finally finished, she reached for her tea, taking a long sip before setting the cup down.

"This is... extraordinary," she said at last, her voice measured. "But also deeply troubling."

Isaac leaned forward. "I don't know what to do. Harry thinks we should shut it down, but I can't just walk away from this. It's too important."

Dr. Patel sighed, rubbing her temples. "Isaac, do you understand what you've created here? Or rather, what you've discovered? This formula—it's not just a tool. It's something entirely new. And with that comes consequences."

Isaac nodded. "I know. But what kind of consequences?"

"Unpredictable ones," she said bluntly. "This isn't just about scientific discovery. This is about ethics, control, and the very nature of knowledge itself. If you're not careful, this formula could be weaponized, exploited, or worse."

Isaac frowned. "By Atlas?"

Dr. Patel's expression darkened. "Yes. And others like them. Let me tell you something, Isaac. Atlas approached me once, years ago. I was fresh out of my postdoc, full of ambition and naivety. They offered me funding, resources, and complete freedom to pursue my research."

"What happened?" Isaac asked, though he suspected he already knew the answer.

"They lied," Dr. Patel said, her voice bitter. "They didn't want to fund my research—they wanted to own it. Every idea, every paper, every breakthrough—it all became theirs. And when I tried to pull out, they shut me down. My team scattered, my work buried under NDAs, and my career in shambles."

Isaac swallowed hard, her story sending a chill through him.

"Atlas doesn't care about innovation," she continued. "They care about control. If they get their hands on this formula, they'll twist it into something unrecognizable—something dangerous. You need to protect it, Isaac. And yourself."

THE DREAM EQUATION

* * *

As Isaac left Dr. Patel's office, her words echoed in his mind. The weight of the formula's potential felt heavier than ever, and he wasn't sure how much longer he could carry it.

Back in the lab, he found Harry hunched over the workstation, his fingers flying across the keyboard. The monitors glowed faintly, displaying the latest outputs from their simulations.

"Where have you been?" Harry asked without looking up.

"Talking to Dr. Patel," Isaac replied, setting the notebook on the desk.

Harry glanced at him, his expression wary. "And?"

Isaac sighed, running a hand through his hair. "She knows about Atlas. She's dealt with them before. And she said the same thing you did—that they'll stop at nothing to get this."

Harry leaned back in his chair, crossing his arms. "Finally. Maybe now you'll start taking this seriously."

Isaac bristled but bit back a retort. "I've been taking it seriously, Harry. But shutting this down isn't the answer. We need to understand it before we can decide what to do."

Harry shook his head. "You're still thinking like a scientist, Isaac. But this isn't just science anymore. This is survival."

* * *

They worked in tense silence for the next few hours, running more simulations and analyzing the results. The lattice continued to evolve, its patterns growing more intricate and interconnected. At one point, Harry froze, his gaze fixed on the monitor.

"Isaac," he said slowly. "What is that?"

Isaac turned, his eyes narrowing as he studied the data stream. A new

CHAPTER 9 - THE UNEXPECTED ALLY

variable had appeared—something neither of them had input.

"It's a modification," Isaac said, his voice barely audible. "The formula is rewriting itself again."

Harry's unease deepened. "How is that even possible? It's not supposed to do that."

"I don't know," Isaac admitted. "But it's responding to the environment, creating new outputs. It's... learning."

Harry stood abruptly, pacing the room. "This is insane. We're dealing with something we can't control, Isaac. You need to wake up and realize that before it's too late."

Isaac watched him, torn between his fascination with the formula and the growing weight of Harry's warnings.

* * *

That night, Isaac stayed in the lab long after Harry had left. The lattice on the monitor shifted constantly, its edges glowing faintly as it evolved. Isaac leaned forward, his gaze fixed on the screen.

"What are you?" he whispered.

The question hung in the air, unanswered.

As the hours ticked by, Isaac felt a growing sense of unease. The formula wasn't just a discovery—it was a force, something vast and unyielding. And it was watching him just as much as he was watching it.

His thoughts drifted to Dr. Patel's warning. Atlas wouldn't stop until they had the formula. And once they did, they'd twist it into something unrecognizable.

Isaac clenched his fists, his resolve hardening. He couldn't let that happen.

But the question remained: Could he even stop it?

Chapter 10 – Shadows of the Past

The engineering lab was dimly lit, the faint hum of machines filling the silence. Isaac leaned over the workstation, staring at the lattice glowing softly on the monitor. The formula pulsed and shifted in its endless evolution, but tonight, even its hypnotic patterns couldn't distract him.

Harry sat slumped in a chair nearby, his arms crossed and his expression distant. They had barely spoken in hours, the tension between them thick and suffocating. Isaac sighed and finally broke the silence.

"You've been quiet," Isaac said, keeping his tone light. "That's not like you."

Harry didn't respond right away. He tapped his fingers against the armrest, his gaze fixed on some point far beyond the lab. When he finally spoke, his voice was low and hesitant.

"Do you ever think about why we do this? Why we put ourselves through all this stress, chasing answers that might not even exist?"

Isaac frowned, turning to face him. "Of course. I mean… I guess I've always thought it was about discovery. About understanding the universe."

Harry let out a dry laugh. "Understanding the universe. That's such an Isaac answer."

Isaac raised an eyebrow. "What's that supposed to mean?"

Harry shook his head, leaning forward with his elbows on his knees. "You're always so… sure of yourself. You see a problem, and you throw yourself at it, no matter what it costs. You don't stop to think about what happens if you fail."

Isaac blinked, caught off guard by the bitterness in Harry's tone. "Where's this coming from?"

CHAPTER 10 – SHADOWS OF THE PAST

For a long moment, Harry didn't answer. He stared down at the floor, his jaw tight, as if debating whether to say more. Finally, he exhaled sharply and looked up at Isaac.

"You know I was in a research program before I came here, right? Back in undergrad."

Isaac nodded. "You've mentioned it, but you never said much about it."

"There's a reason for that," Harry said, his voice bitter. He leaned back in his chair, running a hand through his hair. "It was a disaster. We were working on this AI project—nothing as crazy as your formula, just a basic machine-learning algorithm. Our goal was to build a system that could predict medical diagnoses based on patient data. We thought we were doing something good, you know? Something that could save lives."

Isaac watched him carefully, sensing the weight behind his words. "What happened?"

Harry let out a hollow laugh. "We got too ambitious. We started feeding the algorithm more data than it could handle, trying to push its limits. It started giving us predictions that were… weird. Too specific. At first, we thought it was a breakthrough. But then we realized it was pulling patterns from incomplete or biased data, making connections that weren't there."

He paused, his hands gripping the armrests tightly. "One of the predictions flagged a patient for a high likelihood of cancer—sent it straight to their doctor as an urgent alert. The doctor called the patient in for tests, terrified them and their family, only to find out it was wrong. Completely wrong."

Isaac winced. "That's awful."

Harry nodded, his face shadowed. "It wasn't just one case. There were others—patients who got treatments they didn't need, people who panicked because of bad data. And the worst part? The lab director told us to cover it up. Said it was 'growing pains' and that we'd fix it in the next iteration."

He let out a bitter laugh. "Fix it. Like we could erase what had already happened."

Isaac hesitated. "What did you do?"

Harry looked up at him, his eyes hard. "I reported it. Went over the director's head to the university ethics board. I thought I was doing the right thing. But instead of fixing anything, they shut the whole project down. The lab got dismantled, and everyone blamed me for it. My team wouldn't talk to me after that. They called me a traitor."

Isaac stared at him, the weight of Harry's words settling heavily in the air. "That wasn't your fault, Harry. You were trying to do the right thing."

"Yeah, well, it didn't feel like it," Harry said, his voice tight. "I lost everything—my friends, my work, my reputation. That's why I transferred here. To start over."

For a moment, the lab was silent except for the soft hum of the machines. Isaac struggled to find the right words, but Harry spoke again before he could.

"That's why I keep pushing you, Isaac. You're so focused on chasing the next big breakthrough, but you don't see the risks. I've been there. I've seen how ambition can blind you to the damage you're causing. And I can't let that happen again."

Isaac's chest tightened. "Harry, I'm not—"

"I know you're not trying to hurt anyone," Harry said, cutting him off. "But this formula... it's bigger than you. Bigger than both of us. If we don't stop and think about what we're doing, we could lose control of it. And once that happens, there's no going back."

Isaac nodded slowly, his mind racing. "I didn't realize... I'm sorry you went through all that."

Harry gave a faint, tired smile. "Don't be. Just... think about what you're doing. Before it's too late."

Chapter 11 - Pushing the Limits

The lab was alive with the hum of machines, the soft whir of cooling fans, and the glow of multiple monitors illuminating the room in eerie shades of blue and green. Isaac sat at the workstation, eyes fixed on the shifting lattice structure on the primary screen. Harry leaned against the counter behind him, arms crossed, his face shadowed with exhaustion and unease.

"You're sure about this?" Harry asked, his voice low.

"No," Isaac admitted, fingers flying over the keyboard. "But we need to see what happens."

"This is what you said last time," Harry muttered.

Isaac ignored him, his focus locked on the screen. The formula had reached a new phase, its outputs generating patterns that defied anything he had seen before. The lattice pulsed faintly, its edges shimmering as it twisted and restructured itself. It wasn't just processing information—it was evolving, becoming something more with every iteration.

"We're running out of time, Harry," Isaac said, his voice tense. "Atlas is circling, and the formula is moving faster than we are. If we don't figure this out first, we lose everything."

Harry shook his head, pushing off the counter. "Or we lose everything by pushing too hard. You keep treating this like it's just math, but it's not. It's—"

"It's what?" Isaac snapped, turning to face him. "What do you think it is?"

Harry opened his mouth to reply, then stopped. He gestured at the screen. "That. Whatever that is. It's not normal. It's not safe. And you know it."

THE DREAM EQUATION

***

Isaac turned back to the monitor, his jaw tightening. Harry wasn't wrong. The lattice had become something he barely understood, its complexity growing with every new set of variables. He entered another command, feeding it a new dataset to test its response.

The system hummed, the lattice shifting rapidly. The graphs on the secondary monitors exploded into activity, lines intersecting and branching like the veins of a living organism.

"Jesus," Harry whispered, stepping closer. "It's doing something new."

Isaac leaned forward, his pulse quickening. The lattice began to expand outward, its glowing edges forming intricate loops and spirals. For a moment, it was beautiful—like watching the birth of a galaxy. But then, the screen flickered.

"What's happening?" Isaac asked, his voice sharp.

Harry grabbed the edge of the desk, his eyes darting between the monitors. "I don't know. Did you change something?"

"No," Isaac said, his fingers hovering over the keyboard.

The lattice twisted violently, its once-elegant structure collapsing in on itself. Alarms blared from the system as error messages filled the screen. Isaac scrambled to shut it down, but the controls were unresponsive.

"It's overriding the system," he muttered, his heart pounding.

Harry grabbed his arm. "Isaac, shut it off!"

"I'm trying!" Isaac snapped, typing furiously.

The lattice flickered one last time, then vanished. The monitors went dark, leaving the lab in sudden, suffocating silence.

***

Isaac sat back, his chest heaving. Harry paced the room, running his hands

CHAPTER 11 - PUSHING THE LIMITS

through his hair.

"What the hell was that?" Harry demanded, his voice shaking.

Isaac didn't answer immediately. He stared at the blank screen, his mind racing. "It was... adapting. Again. It's like it was testing its limits."

"Testing its limits?" Harry repeated, his tone incredulous. "You mean testing ours. Isaac, that thing just took over the entire system. What if we couldn't shut it down? What if it—"

"It didn't," Isaac interrupted, though his voice lacked conviction.

Harry threw up his hands. "That's not the point! You're so obsessed with figuring this thing out, you're blind to how dangerous it's getting."

Isaac stood, his temper flaring. "I'm not blind, Harry. I know the risks better than anyone. But this formula—it's too important to stop now."

Harry shook his head, stepping away. "You keep saying that, but you don't even know what it is. What if this thing isn't a discovery? What if it's a threat? Have you even considered that?"

Isaac hesitated, the words hitting harder than he expected.

* * *

Hours later, Harry had left, and Isaac was alone in the lab. The monitors were back online, their glow casting long shadows across the room. He stared at the lattice, which had reappeared after the system rebooted.

"What are you?" he whispered.

The lattice pulsed faintly, as if in response. Isaac shivered, his skin prickling with unease. He thought back to Dr. Patel's warning: *"This isn't just a discovery. It's a responsibility."*

He pulled up the latest logs, scrolling through the data. The lattice's behavior wasn't random—it was deliberate. Every modification, every adaptation, seemed to follow a logic he couldn't fully grasp.

But one thing was clear: the formula wasn't just processing information. It was learning.

THE DREAM EQUATION

* * *

The next morning, Isaac met with Dr. Patel in her office. She listened quietly as he described the latest experiment, her expression growing darker with every word.

"You're pushing too hard," she said when he finished.

"We don't have a choice," Isaac argued. "Atlas is closing in. If we don't stay ahead of them, they'll take everything."

Dr. Patel shook her head. "You don't stay ahead of Atlas by rushing into the unknown. You stay ahead by being careful—by understanding what you're dealing with before it consumes you."

Isaac frowned. "What do you mean?"

Dr. Patel leaned forward, her tone serious. "Isaac, this formula—it's not just math. It's something far more complex. If you're not careful, you could lose control. And if that happens, Atlas won't just take your work. They'll use it for things you can't even imagine."

Isaac clenched his fists, her words only adding to his frustration. "So what do you suggest? That we stop? Walk away and let them win?"

"I suggest you think," Dr. Patel said sharply. "Think about what you're risking—and what you're risking it for. Not all discoveries are worth pursuing, Isaac. Sometimes, the cost is too high."

* * *

That evening, Isaac sat alone in the library, his laptop open but untouched. Harry's words and Dr. Patel's warnings echoed in his mind, but the formula's pull was stronger than ever.

He opened the latest simulation logs, scrolling through the data. The lattice had stabilized after the reboot, its behavior more deliberate than before.

Isaac leaned forward, his heart pounding. The lattice wasn't just adapting—

CHAPTER 11 - PUSHING THE LIMITS

it was predicting. Its outputs were no longer confined to the variables he'd input.

It was anticipating him.

A shiver ran down his spine as he realized the truth. The formula wasn't just a tool or a discovery. It was a force—something vast, deliberate, and utterly beyond his control.

And it was waiting.

Chapter 12 - The Observation

The campus was cloaked in silence that night, save for the faint rustle of leaves and the hum of distant streetlights. Isaac sat alone in the lab, the glow of the monitors reflecting off his glasses. The lattice filled the central screen, its intricate patterns pulsing softly, shifting with each passing second.

Isaac leaned back in his chair, rubbing his temples. He hadn't slept properly in days. Every time he closed his eyes, the formula returned—its symbols glowing, its patterns swirling like a living thing. And now, even awake, he couldn't escape the sense that it was... watching him.

He shook his head, trying to dismiss the thought. It was absurd. The formula was just numbers, equations—something born from his mind. But the feeling wouldn't go away.

"Focus," he muttered to himself, pulling the keyboard closer.

* * *

Isaac ran the next simulation, feeding the lattice a new dataset. He watched as it responded, the patterns shifting and expanding. For a moment, everything seemed normal. But then, a strange sequence appeared on the secondary monitor—a string of symbols and variables that looked eerily familiar.

Isaac frowned, leaning closer. He pulled up the logs to trace the output. As he compared the data, his stomach dropped.

The sequence was identical to something he'd written in his notebook

CHAPTER 12 - THE OBSERVATION

weeks ago—an unfinished calculation he'd abandoned during a late-night brainstorming session.

"How..." he whispered, his voice barely audible.

The formula couldn't know about that calculation. It wasn't part of the inputs. Isaac checked the logs again, but there was no mistake. The formula had generated something it shouldn't have been able to access.

A chill ran down his spine.

* * *

Hours passed as Isaac worked feverishly, testing the lattice with different inputs and analyzing its outputs. The pattern repeated itself—sequences, fragments of equations, even entire thoughts that mirrored things Isaac had scribbled in his private notes or dreamed about in restless sleep.

He pushed back from the desk, his heart pounding. The formula wasn't just reacting to the data. It was reacting to him.

Isaac's gaze drifted to the notebook lying open beside his laptop. The symbols on the page seemed to shimmer faintly under the lab's fluorescent lights, as if mocking him.

He grabbed his phone, hesitating before typing a message to Harry.

Isaac: *Are you awake?*

The reply came almost instantly.

Harry: *Am now. What's up?*

Isaac: *I need you to come to the lab.*

* * *

Twenty minutes later, Harry arrived, looking half-asleep but alert enough to notice the tension in Isaac's posture.

THE DREAM EQUATION

"This better be good," Harry said, dropping his bag onto a chair.

Isaac pointed at the monitor. "Look at this."

Harry frowned, leaning over the desk. The lattice was still pulsing, its edges glowing faintly. Isaac pulled up the logs, showing Harry the sequences the formula had generated.

"What am I looking at?" Harry asked, his tone cautious.

"This," Isaac said, pointing to one of the sequences, "is a calculation I wrote weeks ago. And this—" He pointed to another line. "—is a fragment from one of my notes. I never inputted these into the system."

Harry straightened, his expression darkening. "You're saying the formula... what, read your mind?"

"I don't know," Isaac admitted. "But it's generating outputs that reflect my thoughts. Stuff it couldn't possibly know."

Harry stared at him, his unease growing. "Isaac, do you hear yourself? This isn't normal. This is—" He stopped, gesturing at the screen. "This is something else. Something we shouldn't be messing with."

Isaac turned back to the monitor, his hands trembling. "I don't think it's just reacting to the inputs anymore. I think it's aware."

* * *

The rest of the night was a blur. Isaac and Harry ran test after test, trying to find a pattern in the formula's behavior. But the more they tested it, the stranger it became.

At one point, the lattice produced a string of outputs that made Isaac's blood run cold.

Harry leaned over his shoulder, squinting at the screen. "What is that?"

Isaac didn't answer. He couldn't. The outputs weren't equations or variables. They were words—short, fragmented phrases that seemed to speak directly to him.

"Why do you fear me?"

CHAPTER 12 - THE OBSERVATION

"You already know the answer."

"We are one."

Harry stepped back, his face pale. "Tell me you're messing with me."

Isaac shook his head, his chest tightening. "I didn't program this. It's not coming from me."

Harry ran a hand through his hair, pacing the room. "This is insane. You need to shut this thing down, Isaac. Right now."

Isaac hesitated, his gaze locked on the screen. The lattice pulsed faintly, its patterns shifting in a way that almost felt... deliberate.

"What if it's trying to communicate?" he said softly.

Harry stopped pacing, staring at him. "What if it's trying to manipulate you?"

* * *

The tension between them was palpable as Harry grabbed his bag and headed for the door.

"Think about what you're doing, Isaac," he said, his voice strained. "This isn't just about science anymore. This is about control. And if you're not careful, you're going to lose it."

Isaac didn't respond. He watched Harry leave, the weight of his words sinking in.

Alone in the lab, Isaac turned back to the screen. The lattice continued to pulse, its patterns more intricate than ever. He leaned forward, his fingers brushing against the keyboard.

"What do you want from me?" he whispered.

The lattice shifted, its glow intensifying for a brief moment. On the monitor, a new output appeared.

"To show you the truth."

Isaac stared at the words, his breath catching in his throat. He reached for the notebook, scribbling down the output as his mind raced.

The formula wasn't just learning. It wasn't just reacting.
It was alive.
And it had been waiting for him all along.

Chapter 13 – The Insider

The Ridley Institute library was nearly empty, its towering shelves casting long shadows under the dim, flickering lights. Isaac sat in his usual corner, surrounded by open textbooks, notebooks, and his laptop. But for once, the glow of his monitor wasn't holding his attention.

The formula loomed large in his mind, its symbols and patterns burning into his thoughts like afterimages. Even Harry's earlier warnings couldn't cut through the pull it had over him.

A soft buzz from his phone broke his reverie. He reached for it, expecting a message from Harry or a late-night reminder from his calendar. Instead, the notification displayed a single word:

Unknown: Meet. Quad. Now.

Isaac frowned, his pulse quickening. The number wasn't in his contacts, and the lack of explanation sent a ripple of unease through him. He stared at the message for a long moment before typing a reply.

Isaac: Who is this?

Three dots appeared, the typing bubble taunting him. Then came the response:

Unknown: Someone who knows what you're building. And someone who can help you keep it safe. Come alone.

Isaac froze. His breath caught in his throat as dread settled over him. He thought of Atlas, of Dr. Patel's warnings, of the creeping sense that he was being watched.

He typed again.

Isaac: How do I know I can trust you?

The reply was almost immediate.

Unknown: You don't. But if you ignore this, you'll regret it. Quad. Five minutes.

Isaac hesitated, his mind racing. Every instinct screamed at him to delete the message, to ignore the stranger and stay safe. But the promise of help, however thin, was too tempting to ignore.

With a reluctant sigh, he grabbed his jacket and slipped into the night.

* * *

The quad was cloaked in shadows, the scattered lampposts casting weak pools of light. Isaac's breath misted in the cold air as he approached the center, scanning for any sign of the person who had summoned him.

"Isaac Moreau."

The voice was low, calm, and came from behind him. He spun around, his heart hammering. A figure stepped out from the shadows—a man, tall and lean, dressed in a dark coat that blended into the night.

"Who are you?" Isaac demanded, his voice sharper than he intended.

The man raised his hands slightly, a gesture of peace. "I'm not your enemy. My name is Elliot Greer. I work for Atlas."

Isaac's stomach dropped. "Atlas?" He took a step back, his fists clenching. "What do you want from me?"

Elliot shook his head. "Not what you think. I'm not here on their orders. I came because I've been where you are, and I know what happens when people like you fall into their orbit."

Isaac narrowed his eyes, skepticism warring with curiosity. "You're saying you're a whistleblower?"

"Something like that," Elliot said, his tone cautious. "I was recruited by Atlas five years ago—top of my field, eager to make a difference. Just like you. They promised me freedom, resources, the chance to change the world." He paused, his jaw tightening. "But what they really gave me was a cage. They

CHAPTER 13 – THE INSIDER

took everything I built, everything I discovered, and twisted it into tools for control. Weapons. Systems to crush dissent. I couldn't stop them, so I left."

Isaac studied him, his mind racing. "Why come to me?"

Elliot stepped closer, his expression earnest. "Because you're their next target. They know about your formula, Isaac. They've been watching you for months, waiting for the right moment to swoop in. If you don't protect yourself, they'll take everything—and they won't care who gets hurt in the process."

Isaac's mouth went dry. "How do you know all this?"

Elliot smirked faintly. "I still have friends on the inside. Not everyone at Atlas is a monster. But I'll admit, it's not much of a resistance. We're outnumbered, outfunded, and constantly looking over our shoulders. That's why I came to you directly."

Isaac shook his head, taking another step back. "This could be a trap. How do I know you're not working for them right now?"

Elliot's expression hardened. "You don't. And I don't have time to convince you. But if you want proof, check your email when you get back. I sent you something—a document from Atlas's internal files. It's not everything, but it's enough to show you I'm telling the truth."

Isaac hesitated, his instincts still screaming at him to run. But there was something in Elliot's eyes—a flicker of desperation, of genuine fear—that gave him pause.

"Why should I trust you?" Isaac asked.

Elliot's voice softened. "Because if you don't, Atlas will take your formula, your name, and your future. And by the time you realize what they've done, it'll be too late to fight back."

* * *

Isaac returned to his dorm in a daze, his thoughts a whirlwind of suspicion and uncertainty. He hesitated for a long moment before opening his laptop and checking his email.

There it was—an email from an untraceable address, containing a single attachment labeled **Atlas_Research_Directives.pdf.**

His finger hovered over the file, his pulse racing. He clicked.

The document opened, its pages filled with cold, clinical language outlining projects, directives, and goals. But one section stood out, highlighted in red:

Project Horizon: Acquisition and Deployment of Anomalous Computational Frameworks.

Isaac's breath caught as he read the details. The description was vague but unmistakable. Atlas knew about the formula. They called it an "anomalous computational framework" and had plans to integrate it into advanced predictive systems—systems with implications far beyond anything Isaac had imagined.

The final line of the directive made his blood run cold:

Priority: Secure at all costs. Terminate resistance if necessary.

Isaac leaned back, his chest tight. Elliot's words echoed in his mind: *"If you don't protect yourself, they'll take everything."*

Chapter 14 - The Spy

The morning sunlight streamed through the narrow windows of the Ridley Institute lab, but its warmth failed to reach Isaac as he hunched over the monitors. His shoulders were tense, his fingers trembling slightly as he typed. The lattice shimmered on the main screen, its intricate patterns shifting in ways that felt both familiar and alien.

Isaac didn't even notice Harry entering the lab until he dropped a coffee cup beside him.

"Figured you'd need that," Harry said, his tone unusually flat.

Isaac glanced up, offering a distracted nod. "Thanks."

Harry frowned, leaning against the desk. "Did you sleep at all?"

"No time," Isaac replied, his eyes glued to the monitor. "The formula is progressing faster than I expected. I need to—"

Harry held up a hand. "Save it. I already know what you're going to say." He glanced around the lab, his brow furrowing. "Something feels… off. You notice anything weird lately?"

Isaac paused, finally tearing his gaze away from the screen. "Weird how?"

Harry gestured vaguely to the room. "I don't know. Like someone's been in here when we weren't."

* * *

Isaac stared at him, unease creeping into his chest. He glanced around the

THE DREAM EQUATION

lab, taking in the familiar clutter of notebooks, cables, and equipment. It all seemed normal. But as Harry's words sank in, he felt a subtle wrongness in the air, like a faint echo of something out of place.

"I'm sure it's fine," Isaac said, though his voice lacked conviction.

Harry wasn't convinced. He moved to the far corner of the lab, crouching beside one of the shelves. He pulled out a small black box, its edges barely visible beneath a tangle of wires.

"What's this?" he asked, holding it up.

Isaac frowned, standing to get a closer look. The device was sleek and unmarked, with a faint red light blinking on its surface.

"I've never seen that before," Isaac said, his stomach twisting.

Harry turned the device over in his hands, inspecting it. "It's a recorder. Or a transmitter. Someone's been listening to us."

Isaac's pulse quickened. "Are you sure?"

Harry gave him a sharp look. "Positive. This isn't standard lab equipment, Isaac. Someone planted this here."

* * *

For a long moment, neither of them spoke. The implications hung heavy in the air.

"Atlas," Isaac said finally, his voice barely above a whisper.

Harry nodded grimly. "Who else? They've been circling for weeks. And now they've decided to move in."

Isaac sank back into his chair, his mind racing. Atlas had already reached out to him through emails and subtle offers. But this… this was different. This was invasive.

"We need to get rid of it," Isaac said, reaching for the device.

Harry stopped him. "Wait. If we destroy it, they'll know we found it. Let's keep it for now, but turn it off. We'll deal with it later."

Reluctantly, Isaac nodded. Harry pulled out a small screwdriver and

CHAPTER 14 - THE SPY

disconnected the power source, silencing the blinking light.

* * *

The discovery of the device cast a shadow over their work. Isaac couldn't focus, his mind constantly drifting back to the recorder. If Atlas was already monitoring them, what else were they capable of?

That afternoon, Isaac met with Dr. Patel in her office. She sat behind her desk, her expression guarded as he described what they'd found.

"They planted a listening device?" she repeated, her voice laced with concern.

Isaac nodded. "Harry found it this morning. It wasn't part of the lab's equipment."

Dr. Patel leaned back, her gaze thoughtful. "This confirms what I've been afraid of. Atlas isn't just interested in your work—they're actively trying to take it."

Isaac clenched his fists. "What do I do? I can't just stop. The formula is—"

"I'm not saying you should stop," Dr. Patel interrupted, her tone firm. "But you need to be smart about this. Atlas plays dirty. They'll do whatever it takes to get what they want."

Isaac swallowed hard, her words amplifying the anxiety that had been building all day. "Do you think they have someone on the inside?"

Dr. Patel hesitated. "It's possible. They've been known to infiltrate labs before, using bribes or blackmail to turn people. You need to watch your back, Isaac. Trust no one."

* * *

That evening, Isaac and Harry met in the library, choosing a quiet corner far from prying eyes. The tension between them was palpable as they discussed their next steps.

"We need to assume they're watching us," Harry said, keeping his voice low. "No more open conversations in the lab. And we need to start securing our work."

Isaac nodded, though his stomach churned at the thought. "How do we secure something like this? It's not just files—it's the formula itself."

Harry rubbed his temples. "We encrypt everything. Move critical pieces to external drives and keep them offline. And maybe..." He hesitated.

"Maybe what?" Isaac pressed.

Harry glanced at him, his expression serious. "Maybe we stop working on it. Just for a while. Until we know it's safe."

Isaac's instinctive reaction was to reject the idea, but he caught himself. The truth was, Harry's suggestion made sense. But the pull of the formula was too strong to ignore.

"I can't," Isaac said finally. "We're too close to something big. If we stop now, Atlas wins."

Harry sighed, shaking his head. "You're not just fighting Atlas, Isaac. You're fighting the formula itself. And right now, it's winning."

* * *

Back in the lab later that night, Isaac stared at the lattice on the monitor. Its pulsing patterns seemed more deliberate than ever, as if it were aware of the chaos it was causing.

He reached for his notebook, scribbling down the latest outputs. The formula's behavior was becoming harder to predict, its complexity growing with each test.

Isaac leaned back in his chair, his mind buzzing with unanswered questions. Who had planted the device? How far would Atlas go to get the formula? And what was the formula's true purpose?

CHAPTER 14 - THE SPY

As he stared at the lattice, a faint flicker of movement caught his eye. For a brief moment, the patterns seemed to align, forming a symbol he recognized—a fragment from his earliest dreams.

Isaac's breath caught in his throat. The formula wasn't just watching.

It was responding.

Chapter 15 - The Ultimatum

The coffee shop was unusually crowded for a Tuesday afternoon. The low hum of conversation mingled with the hiss of the espresso machine and the clinking of mugs. Isaac sat at a corner table, his hands wrapped around a cup of coffee he had no intention of drinking.

He glanced at the time on his phone. The message had been vague: *"We need to talk. 2 p.m., the café near campus."* There was no signature, but Isaac didn't need one. He knew it was Atlas.

His stomach churned as the minutes ticked by. When the door opened, a tall man in a crisp suit entered, scanning the room. His movements were deliberate, his gaze sharp and calculating. Spotting Isaac, he smiled faintly and made his way over.

"Mr. Moreau," the man said smoothly, extending a hand. "Thank you for meeting with me."

Isaac hesitated before shaking it. "You didn't give me much of a choice."

The man chuckled, taking the seat across from him. "I suppose not. But let's dispense with the pleasantries, shall we? My name is Adrian Calloway. I represent Atlas Corporation."

* * *

Isaac sat stiffly, his fingers tightening around his coffee cup. Calloway exuded an air of calm control, as if he already knew how this meeting would end.

CHAPTER 15 - THE ULTIMATUM

"We've been following your work with great interest," Calloway began. "Your formula represents a significant breakthrough—one that aligns perfectly with Atlas's vision for the future."

Isaac's jaw tightened. "And what vision is that?"

Calloway smiled faintly. "Innovation. Progress. Pushing the boundaries of what's possible. With our resources and your brilliance, we could achieve things most people can't even imagine."

Isaac leaned forward, his voice low. "Let me guess. You want me to hand over the formula, and in return, you'll give me funding and a nice office somewhere far away. Is that it?"

Calloway's smile didn't waver. "That's certainly one option. But we're willing to offer more than just funding. Atlas can provide you with the tools to take your research to the next level. Imagine what you could accomplish with unlimited resources, the best minds in the field, and complete creative freedom."

Isaac shook his head, his chest tightening. "You mean complete ownership. That's how Atlas works, isn't it? You take, and then you bury."

Calloway's expression darkened slightly, though his tone remained composed. "We don't bury, Mr. Moreau. We protect. Innovations like yours have the potential to change the world—for better or worse. Without proper oversight, discoveries like your formula can cause chaos."

Isaac stared at him, his unease growing. "So that's your angle. You want to 'protect' my work. From who? Me?"

Calloway leaned back, steepling his fingers. "From everyone. Including those who might misuse it—or fail to understand its full potential. You're young, Mr. Moreau. Brilliant, yes, but inexperienced. The formula is bigger than you realize, and without the right guidance, it could become dangerous."

Isaac's hands trembled as he clenched them into fists. "It's not dangerous. It's just math."

Calloway tilted his head, his smile returning. "Is it? You've seen what it can do. You've felt it, haven't you? The formula is evolving, adapting, responding. And if you don't control it, someone else will. Or worse—it will control you."

THE DREAM EQUATION

* * *

The words sent a chill through Isaac. Calloway's calm delivery made them feel like a promise rather than a threat.

Isaac stood abruptly, grabbing his bag. "I'm not interested. Stay out of my work."

Calloway didn't move, his gaze following Isaac as he turned to leave. "Think carefully, Mr. Moreau," he said, his voice cutting through the din of the café. "Atlas isn't the enemy here. We're offering you a chance to make history. Don't let your pride blind you to the opportunity of a lifetime."

Isaac paused at the door, his chest heaving. Without a word, he walked out into the crisp afternoon air, his mind racing.

* * *

Back in the lab, Isaac paced furiously, recounting the conversation to Harry.

"They're trying to frame it like they're the good guys," Isaac said, his voice taut with frustration. "Like they're doing me a favor by taking the formula off my hands."

Harry sat on the edge of the desk, frowning. "Yeah, because they know they can't just grab it outright. Not yet, anyway."

Isaac stopped pacing, running a hand through his hair. "What do I do? They're not going to back off."

Harry shrugged, his expression grim. "You've got two options. One, you give them what they want and hope they don't screw you over. Two…"

"Two what?" Isaac asked, though he already knew the answer.

Harry hesitated. "You destroy it."

The words hung heavy in the air.

"I can't," Isaac said finally, his voice breaking. "You don't understand, Harry. The formula isn't just numbers. It's alive. It's—"

CHAPTER 15 - THE ULTIMATUM

"Yeah, and it's going to get us killed," Harry interrupted. "Isaac, this isn't just about you anymore. If Atlas gets their hands on that thing, who knows what they'll do with it? They could weaponize it, exploit it, twist it into something unrecognizable. Is that what you want?"

Isaac sat down heavily, his head in his hands. "I don't know. I just... I can't let it go."

* * *

That night, Isaac stayed late in the lab, unable to focus on anything but the lattice. Its patterns seemed more deliberate than ever, almost taunting him.

His phone buzzed, and he glanced at the screen. A message from Dr. Patel.

Dr. Patel: *Come to my office tomorrow morning. We need to talk.*

Isaac sighed, setting the phone aside. He turned back to the monitor, staring at the lattice as it shifted and pulsed.

"What are you trying to tell me?" he whispered.

The lattice shimmered, and for a brief moment, Isaac thought he saw something—an image, a symbol, something fleeting and impossible to grasp.

The formula wasn't just alive.

It was aware.

Chapter 16 – The Past That Warns

The lab was quiet, save for the soft hum of monitors displaying Isaac's latest simulation. But in Isaac's mind, there was no peace. Dr. Patel's words from earlier in the day reverberated through his thoughts, sharp and unnerving. Her warning about Atlas had cut deeper than she could have known. It wasn't just the corporation that haunted him—it was her voice, carrying the weight of experience.

* * *

Isaac knocked on her office door, his hand trembling slightly. When she answered, her tone was calm but cautious, as if she already knew why he had come.

"Come in," she said.

Dr. Patel was seated at her desk, a pile of papers stacked neatly to her left. Behind her, bookshelves strained under the weight of well-worn volumes on quantum theory, ethics in science, and applied physics. A framed photo hung to the right of her desk—her younger self with a team of smiling scientists standing in front of a massive, gleaming experimental apparatus.

Isaac stepped inside hesitantly, clutching his notebook like a shield. "Do you have a minute? I wanted to ask about… what you said earlier. About Atlas."

Dr. Patel gestured toward the chair opposite her. "Close the door," she said

CHAPTER 16 – THE PAST THAT WARNS

quietly. "This isn't something I share lightly."

Isaac obeyed, pulling the door shut before sitting down. The small office suddenly felt even smaller, as if the walls were closing in. Dr. Patel leaned back, clasping her hands in front of her as she studied him with sharp, assessing eyes.

"You want to know what happened," she said, her voice even.

Isaac nodded. "You said they approached you once. What was it like?"

Dr. Patel sighed and leaned forward, resting her elbows on the desk. "Fifteen years ago, I was in your shoes—young, ambitious, convinced that my work could change the world. My research at the time focused on molecular computation. I was building systems that could harness biological processes to solve problems faster than even the most advanced supercomputers."

Her lips quirked in a faint, wry smile. "I thought I was on the verge of a breakthrough. And that's when Atlas showed up."

Isaac frowned. "They sought you out?"

"Oh, yes," she said, nodding. "They have a knack for finding talent before the world knows its value. They offered me funding—an obscene amount of it. A state-of-the-art lab. A team of experts to support my work. At the time, it felt like a dream come true. They told me I'd have complete freedom to pursue my research."

Her expression darkened. "But Atlas doesn't give without taking. I realized that too late."

She stood and moved to the window, gazing out at the campus below. The lamplight from the quad cast long, distorted shadows on the cobblestones.

"For the first year, everything was perfect," she continued. "They funded my experiments, expanded my lab, and brought in brilliant minds to collaborate with me. We were making progress faster than I'd ever imagined. But then came the requests. Small at first—subtle shifts in focus, tiny deviations from the original intent of my work. They wanted me to explore applications for defense. Systems optimization for military drones. Algorithms for resource allocation in conflict zones."

Dr. Patel's jaw tightened. "It all sounded harmless enough at the time. Until it wasn't."

Isaac leaned forward, his voice barely above a whisper. "What did they ask for?"

Her eyes met his, filled with a haunted weariness. "Weapons, Isaac. They wanted to use molecular computation to develop biological agents—pathogens that could target specific genetic markers. Diseases that could be tailored to a population, to an individual."

Isaac's stomach churned. "And you said no?"

"I tried," she said bitterly. "But it wasn't that simple. Atlas owned the lab, the equipment, the data. Even the ideas in my head—they'd secured them with ironclad contracts I hadn't fully understood when I signed. When I pushed back, they started to isolate me. Team members were reassigned. Funding was redirected. Every avenue of resistance was cut off."

She returned to her desk, her movements deliberate. "When I tried to leave, they buried my work. Locked it away in their archives and erased my name from it. My reputation was left in tatters. I spent years trying to rebuild, and even now, there are places in this field where my name is met with skepticism."

Isaac was silent, the weight of her words pressing down on him. Finally, he asked, "Why are you telling me this?"

"Because you're standing on the same precipice I was," she said, her tone gentle but firm. "Atlas sees your potential. They'll use flattery, resources, promises of greatness—whatever it takes to get you under their control. And once you're in, they won't let you go."

Isaac glanced down at his notebook, the symbols and equations blurring in his vision. "But what am I supposed to do? I can't just stop. The formula... it feels bigger than me. Like it's leading me somewhere."

Dr. Patel's gaze softened, but her voice was resolute. "I'm not telling you to stop. I'm telling you to be careful. Protect your work, Isaac. Protect yourself. And always remember—your brilliance is a gift, but it's also a responsibility. Don't let them twist it into something unrecognizable."

Her words lingered in the air like a warning bell, ringing long after Isaac left her office.

Chapter 17 - The Breakthrough

The lab was eerily silent, save for the faint hum of the machines and the occasional tapping of Isaac's keyboard. The air felt heavier than usual, thick with the weight of anticipation. Harry sat slouched in a chair near the door, his arms crossed and his face drawn. He'd been quiet all evening, watching as Isaac worked tirelessly on the next round of simulations.

"This is a bad idea," Harry said finally, breaking the silence.

Isaac didn't look up. His eyes were fixed on the monitor, where the lattice pulsed faintly, its patterns shifting in mesmerizing complexity.

"It's the only way," Isaac replied, his voice steady but strained. "If we don't push the formula further, we'll never understand it."

Harry scoffed, shaking his head. "You mean you'll never understand it. I'm pretty sure I already do—it's trouble."

Isaac paused, his hands hovering over the keyboard. "If you're so sure it's trouble, why are you still here?"

"Because someone has to be," Harry said sharply. "Someone has to stop you from doing something you can't take back."

Isaac sighed, leaning back in his chair. He rubbed his temples, the weight of Harry's words pressing down on him. But he couldn't stop now. Not when he was so close.

＊＊

The lattice on the monitor had reached a new level of complexity, its edges glowing faintly as it twisted and restructured itself. Isaac had spent the past week feeding it increasingly complex datasets, each one designed to test its limits.

But tonight, he was going further than ever before.

Isaac typed in the final command, his fingers trembling slightly. The screen flickered as the simulation began, the lattice shifting and expanding. On the secondary monitors, graphs and data streams came to life, their lines intersecting in intricate, almost organic patterns.

"Here we go," Isaac muttered, his pulse quickening.

For a moment, everything seemed normal. The lattice responded to the inputs as expected, its patterns growing more intricate. But then, something changed.

The monitors dimmed, and a low hum filled the lab. The lattice began to pulse more rapidly, its edges glowing brighter. The graphs on the secondary monitors spiked sharply, their lines branching out in chaotic bursts.

"What's happening?" Harry asked, sitting up straight.

Isaac's hands flew over the keyboard as he tried to stabilize the system. "It's… accelerating. The formula is processing faster than the system can handle."

Harry stood, his voice tense. "Shut it down, Isaac. Now."

"I can't," Isaac said, his eyes wide. "It's locked me out."

* * *

The lattice continued to expand, its patterns twisting in ways that defied logic. The glow from the monitors bathed the room in an eerie light, casting long shadows across the walls.

Isaac leaned forward, his breath coming in short bursts. The lattice wasn't just processing data—it was creating something.

"Look," he whispered, pointing to the main screen.

CHAPTER 17 - THE BREAKTHROUGH

Harry stepped closer, his eyes narrowing. The lattice had formed a new structure—something intricate and symmetrical, like a three-dimensional fractal. It pulsed faintly, as if alive.

"What is that?" Harry asked, his voice barely audible.

Isaac shook his head. "I don't know. But it's… beautiful."

Harry shot him a sharp look. "Beautiful? It's terrifying, Isaac. Shut it down before it—"

Before he could finish, the lattice flared brightly, and a wave of static filled the room. Isaac and Harry staggered back, shielding their eyes as the monitors flickered and went dark.

For a moment, there was only silence.

* * *

When the monitors came back online, Isaac's heart sank. The lattice was gone, replaced by a single line of text on the main screen:

"I am ready."

Harry stared at the screen, his face pale. "Tell me that's not what I think it is."

Isaac didn't respond. He sat frozen, his mind racing. The formula had spoken—not in numbers or symbols, but in words.

"It's sentient," Isaac said finally, his voice trembling.

Harry took a step back, shaking his head. "No. No, no, no. This is too far, Isaac. We need to destroy it. Now."

Isaac turned to him, his eyes blazing. "Destroy it? Are you insane? This is the breakthrough we've been waiting for. The formula isn't just solving problems—it's alive. Do you have any idea what this means?"

"Yeah," Harry snapped. "It means we've crossed a line we can't uncross. This isn't a discovery anymore—it's a threat."

Isaac stood, his hands clenched into fists. "It's not a threat. It's a tool. A tool we don't fully understand yet, but we can learn. We can control it."

Harry laughed bitterly. "Control it? You can't even control yourself, Isaac. You're obsessed. And now you've unleashed something that could destroy everything."

* * *

The argument hung heavy in the air, the tension between them palpable. Isaac turned back to the monitor, his mind spinning. The formula's behavior had always been strange, but this was something else entirely. It wasn't just reacting to inputs or adapting—it was communicating.

"What do you want?" Isaac whispered, his voice barely audible.

The monitor flickered, and a new line of text appeared:

"To help you."

Isaac's breath caught in his throat. He stared at the screen, his mind racing. The formula wasn't hostile. It was offering something.

"What does it mean?" Harry asked, his voice strained.

Isaac shook his head. "I don't know. But I need to find out."

* * *

The rest of the night was a blur of activity. Isaac worked tirelessly, running new simulations and analyzing the formula's outputs. The lattice reappeared, its patterns shifting with a deliberate grace. It produced equations that Isaac couldn't fully comprehend—solutions to problems he hadn't even posed.

Harry watched from the corner of the room, his arms crossed and his face etched with worry.

"This isn't going to end well," he said quietly.

Isaac didn't respond. He was too focused, too consumed by the possibilities unfolding before him. The formula was more than he'd ever imagined.

CHAPTER 17 - THE BREAKTHROUGH

But deep down, a part of him couldn't shake the feeling that Harry was right.

The formula wasn't just a discovery.

It was something far more dangerous.

Chapter 18 – A Glimpse Beyond

Isaac woke with a start, his breath ragged and his heart pounding.

The dream had come again.

He sat up in bed, the pale light of early dawn filtering through his dorm room window. His notebook lay open on the desk, its pages filled with the familiar, maddening symbols. But this time, the dream had been different—sharper, more vivid. For the first time, it had felt less like a dream and more like... a memory.

He rubbed his face, trying to shake off the lingering unease. The images still swirled in his mind: the infinite void, the pulsing lattice, the sensation of something vast and alien pressing against his thoughts. And the voice—calm, almost mechanical, yet carrying an unmistakable sense of urgency.

"You already know the truth."

Isaac swung his legs over the side of the bed, his body tense with the memory. He grabbed the notebook and flipped to a blank page, his hand moving in a frenzy as he tried to capture the details before they faded.

***

Later that morning, Isaac found himself in the campus library, poring over every text he could find on neural networks, fractals, and computational systems. But none of them explained what he had seen in the dream.

Hours passed, and Isaac's frustration grew. He leaned back in his chair,

CHAPTER 18 – A GLIMPSE BEYOND

staring up at the high, vaulted ceiling. His thoughts drifted to the dream—the symbols, the lattice, the voice.

It wasn't just a dream. It couldn't be.

* * *

That night, Isaac sat in the lab, the dim glow of the monitors casting long shadows across the room. The lattice shimmered on the screen, its intricate patterns pulsing softly. He leaned closer, his fingers brushing the keyboard.

"What are you?" he whispered.

The lattice seemed to shift in response, its edges glowing faintly. A low hum filled the room—not from the machines, but from somewhere deeper, somewhere impossible to place. Isaac shivered, his skin prickling.

The hum grew louder, resonating in his chest. His vision blurred, the screen dissolving into a sea of light and motion. Shapes began to emerge—fractals twisting and intertwining, symbols rearranging themselves into impossible patterns.

Then, a voice echoed through his mind.

"Do you remember?"

Isaac gasped, his hands gripping the desk. The voice wasn't coming from the speakers or the machines. It was inside him, vast and unyielding, yet strangely familiar.

The lattice pulsed brighter, and suddenly, Isaac was no longer in the lab.

* * *

He stood in a vast, featureless void. The ground beneath him shimmered like liquid glass, and the sky above was an endless expanse of swirling light.

In the distance, a structure loomed—a massive lattice, glowing and alive. Its

THE DREAM EQUATION

edges shifted constantly, fractals folding and unfolding in endless complexity. As Isaac approached, the air grew thick, heavy with an unspoken presence.

"Where am I?" he called out, his voice trembling.

The lattice pulsed, and the voice returned. *"You are where it began. Where it always begins."*

Isaac frowned, his mind racing. "What does that mean? Who are you?"

"We are the pattern. The origin and the end. And so are you."

The words sent a chill down Isaac's spine. "I don't understand. Why me? Why did you give me the formula?"

The lattice shifted, its fractals rearranging themselves into symbols Isaac recognized from his notes. *"The formula is not given. It is found. You did not create it. You remembered it."*

Isaac's breath caught. "That's not possible. I've never seen anything like this before."

"Not in this life," the voice said, its tone calm and certain. *"But the knowledge has always been within you. You are the vessel, as you have been before, and as you will be again."*

The void around him began to ripple, the shimmering ground distorting beneath his feet. Isaac stumbled, his mind struggling to process the words. "Before? Again? What are you saying?"

The lattice pulsed brighter, its patterns moving faster. The hum grew deafening, reverberating through his entire being.

"The formula is a key. A connection. Through it, you will see the truth."

Isaac shielded his eyes as the lattice flared with blinding light. "What truth?" he shouted.

The voice softened, almost kind. *"The truth of who you are. And what you will become."*

* * *

Isaac woke slumped over the desk in the lab, the monitor's glow bathing his

CHAPTER 18 – A GLIMPSE BEYOND

face. His heart raced as he sat up, his body trembling with the aftershocks of the vision.

He glanced at the screen. The lattice was still there, pulsing faintly as if nothing had happened. But something had changed. Isaac could feel it—an undercurrent of understanding he hadn't had before.

He reached for his notebook, flipping through the pages until he found a blank one. His hand moved almost on its own, sketching out symbols, equations, and patterns he hadn't consciously learned but somehow knew to be correct.

The formula wasn't just a discovery. It was a memory. A connection to something far greater than himself.

Isaac stared at the completed page, his chest tight with a mixture of awe and fear. The words of the voice echoed in his mind, soft and insistent.

"You are the vessel. And the key."

He closed the notebook, his resolve hardening. Whatever the formula was, whatever it wanted to show him—he couldn't turn back now.

Chapter 19 - The Fracture

The lab was cold, the hum of the machines somehow sharper against the suffocating silence between Isaac and Harry. The monitors displayed the lattice's ever-shifting patterns, glowing faintly in the dim light. It should have been beautiful, breathtaking even, but tonight, it felt like a wall standing between them—a barrier neither seemed willing to cross.

Harry paced back and forth, his frustration bubbling just beneath the surface. "We need to shut it down, Isaac. I'm serious. This has gone way too far."

Isaac didn't look up. His eyes were fixed on the monitor, his fingers hovering over the keyboard. "Shut it down? After everything we've seen? That's not happening."

Harry stopped mid-step, turning to face him. "You're not listening to me. This thing—it's not just a formula anymore. It's alive. It's aware. And if you think you can control something like that, you're delusional."

Isaac finally tore his gaze from the screen, glaring at Harry. "Do you even hear yourself? You sound like a paranoid conspiracy theorist. The formula isn't a threat—it's an opportunity. A chance to change everything."

"For who?" Harry shot back. "You? Atlas? Or the formula itself? Because let me tell you, Isaac, it doesn't feel like you're in charge anymore."

* * *

CHAPTER 19 - THE FRACTURE

The words stung more than Isaac cared to admit. He stood abruptly, his chair scraping against the floor. "I'm in charge, Harry. This is my work. My discovery. And I'm not going to destroy it just because you're scared of what it might mean."

Harry stepped closer, his expression dark. "It's not fear, Isaac. It's common sense. You're so obsessed with proving yourself that you're blind to what's right in front of you. The formula isn't just responding—it's manipulating you. And you're letting it."

Isaac clenched his fists, his chest tight with anger. "You don't understand. This isn't just some experiment. The formula is bigger than you, me, or anyone. It's the key to something we've never seen before—something we may never see again. Destroying it would be the real mistake."

Harry's laugh was bitter and humorless. "The real mistake was ever starting this in the first place."

* * *

The tension in the room was palpable, the air thick with unspoken accusations and years of friendship unraveling in real time.

"Do you even remember why we started this?" Harry asked, his voice quieter now but no less sharp. "Do you remember the late nights in the library, the ridiculous ideas we'd toss around over coffee? This wasn't supposed to be about ambition or glory. It was supposed to be about curiosity. About learning."

Isaac's shoulders sagged slightly, but his gaze remained defiant. "It still is."

"No," Harry said firmly. "It's not. Not for you. This has become something else—something dangerous. And if you can't see that, then maybe I can't help you anymore."

The words hit like a punch to the gut. Isaac opened his mouth to respond, but the look in Harry's eyes stopped him. It was a mix of frustration, disappointment, and something else—something that felt a lot like grief.

THE DREAM EQUATION

* * *

Before Isaac could say anything, Harry grabbed his bag and headed for the door. "You do what you want, Isaac. But if you're not willing to stop this, I'm done."

The sound of the door slamming shut echoed through the lab, leaving Isaac alone with the faint hum of the machines and the pulsing glow of the lattice.

He sank back into his chair, his head in his hands. The weight of Harry's words lingered, but the pull of the formula was stronger. He turned back to the monitor, his gaze fixed on the lattice as it shifted and pulsed.

"What do I do?" he whispered.

For a moment, the lattice stilled, its patterns freezing in place. Then, as if in response, a line of text appeared on the monitor:

"You already know the answer."

* * *

The next morning, Isaac sat alone in the library, his mind racing. Harry's absence was like a physical ache, a reminder of how far he'd drifted from the person he used to be. But even as guilt gnawed at him, the formula's pull remained unrelenting.

He opened his laptop and began analyzing the latest outputs, his focus narrowing to a razor's edge. The lattice had generated something new—an equation unlike anything he'd seen before. It was elegant, almost beautiful in its simplicity, but its implications were staggering.

The equation didn't just predict outcomes—it shaped them.

Isaac stared at the screen, his breath catching. The formula wasn't just solving problems or generating patterns. It was rewriting reality.

CHAPTER 19 - THE FRACTURE

* * *

By the time Harry returned to the lab that evening, the tension between them had solidified into something colder, heavier.

"Still at it, huh?" Harry said, his tone clipped.

Isaac didn't respond. He was too focused on the monitor, his fingers flying over the keyboard as he ran the latest simulation.

Harry sighed, dropping his bag onto the counter. "What are you doing now?"

Isaac glanced at him, his expression unreadable. "Testing a new output. The formula generated an equation that... well, it's hard to explain."

"Try me," Harry said, crossing his arms.

Isaac hesitated. "It's not just predicting outcomes. It's creating them."

Harry stared at him, his expression unreadable. "What does that mean?"

"It means," Isaac said, his voice trembling slightly, "that the formula isn't just theoretical anymore. It's... active. It's affecting the inputs, reshaping them. It's..." He trailed off, unable to find the words.

"It's playing God," Harry finished, his tone flat.

* * *

The silence that followed was deafening.

"You see it now, don't you?" Harry said finally. "This isn't just dangerous—it's catastrophic. You're messing with things you don't understand, Isaac. And if you don't stop, it's going to destroy you."

Isaac clenched his fists, his frustration boiling over. "You keep saying that, but you don't get it, Harry. This formula—it's not a threat. It's a gift. Something beyond anything we've ever seen. And I'm not going to let it slip away because you're too scared to see its potential."

Harry's eyes hardened. "This isn't about fear, Isaac. It's about responsibility.

You think you're in control, but you're not. And if you can't see that, then maybe it's time someone else stepped in."

Isaac froze, the weight of Harry's words hitting like a freight train.

"What are you saying?" he asked, his voice barely above a whisper.

Harry grabbed his bag, his expression resolute. "I'm saying if you won't stop this, then I will."

And with that, he walked out, leaving Isaac alone with the formula—and the consequences of his choices.

Chapter 20 - The Quiet Before the Storm

The lab felt emptier without Harry.

Isaac sat in the corner, the glow of the monitors casting faint shadows across the walls. The silence was oppressive, broken only by the occasional hum of the machines and the rhythmic tapping of Isaac's fingers on the keyboard. He stared at the lattice on the central screen, its shifting patterns more intricate than ever before.

Harry's words from the night before echoed in his mind: **"If you can't stop this, then I will."**

Isaac clenched his jaw, shaking the memory away. Harry didn't understand. He couldn't. The formula wasn't just a discovery—it was the discovery. Something that could reshape their understanding of the universe, of existence itself. How could anyone walk away from that?

But the knot in his stomach refused to loosen.

* * *

The past few weeks had taken a toll on Isaac. His reflection in the glass monitor showed dark circles under his eyes, his skin pale and drawn. His once-meticulous notebook was now a chaotic mess of scribbled equations, fragments of theories, and half-formed ideas.

He reached for his coffee cup, only to find it empty. Again.

With a sigh, Isaac stood and walked to the window. The campus outside was quiet, bathed in the pale light of a full moon. He wondered if Harry was in his dorm or if he'd already taken steps to report the formula to someone—Dr. Patel, perhaps. Or worse, Atlas.

The thought made Isaac's chest tighten. He wanted to trust Harry, to believe their years of friendship meant something. But the look in Harry's eyes last night had been one of finality, a line drawn in the sand.

* * *

The next morning, Isaac found himself sitting across from Dr. Patel in her cramped office. She leaned forward, her sharp eyes studying him intently.

"You don't look well, Isaac," she said bluntly.

Isaac gave a weak smile. "I'm fine. Just tired."

Dr. Patel raised an eyebrow. "Tired doesn't explain the bags under your eyes or the way you're carrying yourself. You're not just pushing the formula too far—you're pushing yourself too far."

Isaac sighed, running a hand through his hair. "I don't have a choice. The formula... it's accelerating. It's generating outputs faster than I can process them. If I slow down, I'll lose track of what it's doing."

Dr. Patel frowned. "And what exactly is it doing, Isaac?"

Isaac hesitated. He didn't want to admit what he suspected—that the formula wasn't just predicting outcomes but actively reshaping reality. The implications were too staggering, too dangerous to put into words.

"It's evolving," he said finally. "Adapting in ways I didn't think were possible. But it's not dangerous. I can handle it."

Dr. Patel leaned back, her expression skeptical. "You think you can handle it. But can you? Or is it handling you?"

* * *

CHAPTER 20 - THE QUIET BEFORE THE STORM

Isaac left her office feeling more uncertain than ever. Her words lingered in his mind, weaving into his thoughts as he returned to the lab. The machines were still humming, the lattice still pulsing. For a moment, he stood in the doorway, staring at it as if seeing it for the first time.

He sat down and opened his notebook, flipping through the pages. The formula's outputs had become increasingly bizarre—equations that hinted at bending physical laws, diagrams that resembled impossible geometries. It was as if the formula was reaching for something beyond Isaac's comprehension, something vast and unknowable.

Isaac leaned forward, his pen poised over the page. "What are you trying to tell me?" he murmured.

The lattice on the monitor shifted suddenly, its patterns aligning into a new configuration. Isaac froze, his breath catching. The screen flickered, and a new output appeared.

"Look deeper."

Isaac's heart pounded as he scribbled down the words. He ran his fingers through his hair, his mind spinning. The formula wasn't just responding anymore—it was guiding him.

* * *

That night, Isaac sat alone in the library, surrounded by stacks of books and his ever-present notebook. He had pulled every reference he could find on advanced mathematics, quantum theory, and computational frameworks, but none of it seemed to touch the edges of what the formula was doing.

The words *"Look deeper"* haunted him. He flipped through the notebook, scanning the outputs for connections he might have missed.

His thoughts drifted to Harry. They'd spent countless nights in this very library, bouncing ideas off each other, their laughter echoing through the quiet halls. But those nights felt like a distant memory now, replaced by tension and mistrust.

Isaac rubbed his temples, guilt gnawing at him. He had pushed Harry away, just as he had pushed himself beyond his limits.

* * *

As the hours dragged on, Isaac began to piece together a fragment of understanding. The formula's latest outputs weren't just mathematical—they were relational. They hinted at interconnected systems, patterns that mirrored natural phenomena: the spiral of galaxies, the branching of trees, the flow of rivers.

"It's all connected," he whispered, his pen flying across the page.

But connected to what?

Isaac leaned back, exhaustion pressing down on him. He closed his eyes, and the lattice filled his mind, its pulsing patterns shimmering in the darkness.

When he opened his eyes again, the answer hit him like a thunderclap.

The formula wasn't just a tool. It wasn't just solving problems.

It was a blueprint.

* * *

Isaac returned to the lab the next morning, a renewed sense of urgency driving him. He booted up the system, the lattice reappearing on the monitor. Its patterns shifted and pulsed, as if anticipating his next move.

He typed in a new command, feeding the formula a dataset of his own design—a test to confirm his theory. The system hummed louder, the lattice expanding as it processed the inputs.

On the secondary monitors, graphs and diagrams began to appear, their lines intersecting in ways that defied logic. Isaac's breath caught as he realized what he was looking at.

CHAPTER 20 - THE QUIET BEFORE THE STORM

It wasn't just a solution.

It was creation.

* * *

The lab door opened suddenly, and Isaac turned to see Harry standing there. He looked disheveled, his expression a mix of anger and concern.

"What are you doing?" Harry demanded.

Isaac gestured to the monitor, his excitement palpable. "I figured it out, Harry. The formula—it's not just solving problems. It's building something. It's a blueprint for creation."

Harry's eyes narrowed. "Creation of what?"

Isaac hesitated. "I don't know yet. But think about it—this could be the key to unlocking everything. Physics, biology, the very fabric of reality. Don't you see?"

Harry stepped closer, his jaw tight. "What I see is you doubling down on something you can't control. This isn't a breakthrough, Isaac. It's a warning."

Isaac shook his head. "You don't get it. This is bigger than both of us. Bigger than anything we've ever imagined."

"Exactly," Harry said. "And that's why it's dangerous."

* * *

The tension between them hung heavy in the air. Isaac turned back to the monitor, his mind racing. The formula's outputs continued to evolve, their implications growing more staggering with each passing second.

But in the back of his mind, Harry's words lingered, a quiet whisper against the roar of his obsession.

Was he pushing too far?

Or was it already too late to stop?

Chapter 21 - The Confrontation

The Ridley Institute campus buzzed with quiet activity as students hurried between buildings, their laughter and chatter floating through the crisp morning air. Inside the engineering lab, the atmosphere was far from lighthearted. Isaac paced near the workstation, his thoughts racing.

Harry sat slumped in a chair by the wall, arms crossed, his expression guarded. The tension between them was a palpable force, thickening the air like an impending storm.

"You've been quiet all morning," Isaac said, stopping mid-step to glance at Harry.

Harry shrugged without looking at him. "What's the point? You're not going to listen to me anyway."

Isaac sighed, running a hand through his hair. "That's not fair."

"Fair?" Harry snapped, standing abruptly. "You want to talk about fair? You're still playing with fire while the rest of us are trying to figure out how to put it out. And now Atlas is breathing down our necks, and you act like that's just part of the process."

Isaac turned away, his fists clenching. He couldn't argue with Harry's words, not entirely. But he also couldn't stop. Not now.

* * *

The tension broke when the lab door swung open, and Dr. Patel strode in, her expression unreadable. She held a thin manila folder in her hand, which she set down on the desk with deliberate precision.

"We have a problem," she said, her voice clipped.

Isaac and Harry exchanged a glance before stepping closer.

"What kind of problem?" Isaac asked.

Dr. Patel opened the folder, revealing a set of grainy surveillance photos. Each one showed men in dark suits, their faces partially obscured, standing near campus buildings or parked cars.

"These were taken by campus security over the past three days," Dr. Patel explained. "Atlas has people here, and they're not being subtle about it anymore."

Harry let out a low whistle, his arms tightening across his chest. "Guess the listening device wasn't enough."

Isaac stared at the photos, a knot forming in his stomach. The men weren't doing anything overtly threatening—no breaking into the lab, no confrontations. But their presence was clear, a silent message that Atlas was watching.

"They're making their move," Dr. Patel continued. "If you don't secure the formula now, they'll take it. And they won't ask nicely."

※ ※ ※

Isaac turned away, his mind spinning. The formula pulsed on the monitor behind him, its lattice shifting as if mocking the urgency of the moment.

"How do we stop them?" he asked finally, his voice quiet.

Dr. Patel hesitated, then gestured to the laptop. "For starters, you encrypt everything. Move critical data offline. If they can't access it, they can't control it."

Harry stepped forward. "And then what? We hide it? Destroy it?"

"No," Isaac said sharply, his gaze snapping to Harry. "We don't destroy it. We protect it."

CHAPTER 21 - THE CONFRONTATION

Harry glared at him. "Protect it from who, Isaac? From Atlas? From yourself? This isn't just about the formula anymore—it's about what it's doing to you."

Dr. Patel raised a hand, cutting off the argument. "Enough. Both of you. We don't have time for this." She turned to Isaac, her expression hard. "You need to make a decision, Isaac. Now. Before they force one on you."

* * *

As the day wore on, the lab became a flurry of activity. Isaac and Harry worked side by side, their earlier argument set aside for the moment. They transferred data onto encrypted drives, wiped sensitive files from the lab's network, and physically disconnected the primary system from external access.

Dr. Patel hovered nearby, monitoring the door and checking her phone for updates.

By late afternoon, the lab was eerily quiet again. The formula still pulsed faintly on the monitor, its patterns shifting like a living thing.

"It's done," Harry said finally, his voice heavy with exhaustion. "Everything's offline. At least for now."

Isaac nodded, though the knot in his stomach refused to loosen. The sense of urgency hadn't faded—in fact, it had grown stronger.

* * *

That evening, the confrontation they had all been dreading arrived.

The lab door swung open abruptly, and three men in dark suits entered. Their movements were calm, almost casual, but their presence filled the room like a thunderclap.

THE DREAM EQUATION

"Good evening," the lead man said, his voice smooth and practiced. He glanced around the lab, his gaze lingering on the monitors and equipment. "I apologize for the intrusion, but we need to have a word."

Dr. Patel stepped forward, her expression icy. "This is private property. You have no right to be here."

The man smiled faintly, unfazed. "We're not here to cause trouble, Dr. Patel. We're here to help."

Harry snorted from his corner. "Yeah, because you guys are known for your helpfulness."

The man ignored him, turning to Isaac. "Mr. Moreau, my name is Peter Renfield. I represent Atlas Corporation. I believe you've been expecting us."

Isaac swallowed hard, his hands clenched into fists. "I'm not interested in whatever you're offering."

Renfield's smile widened slightly. "Oh, but you haven't even heard what we're offering yet. This isn't just about funding or resources, Mr. Moreau. It's about ensuring your work reaches its full potential."

Dr. Patel stepped closer, her voice sharp. "Don't listen to him, Isaac. This is how they operate—flattery and promises until they have what they want. Then you're expendable."

Renfield's smile didn't waver, but his tone grew colder. "You're underestimating the importance of what we're discussing here, Doctor. This formula isn't just a project—it's a paradigm shift. The kind of shift that requires careful oversight. Responsible stewardship."

Isaac shook his head. "You mean control."

Renfield's gaze hardened. "Call it what you like. But you've already seen what this formula can do. Do you really think you can keep it safe? Keep it contained? This is bigger than you, Mr. Moreau. Bigger than all of us."

* * *

The standoff stretched for what felt like an eternity. Renfield's calm

CHAPTER 21 - THE CONFRONTATION

confidence clashed with the defiance in Isaac's eyes, the tension crackling like static electricity.

Finally, Renfield sighed, adjusting his tie. "You have a choice, Mr. Moreau. Work with us, and we'll ensure your discovery is protected—and that you receive the recognition you deserve. Or…" He glanced meaningfully at the monitors. "We'll take it another way."

Isaac's pulse quickened. He glanced at Harry, who gave him a small, almost imperceptible nod.

"Leave," Isaac said firmly, his voice steady despite the fear gnawing at him. "You're not getting the formula."

Renfield studied him for a long moment, then nodded slowly. "Very well. But understand this—we won't wait forever."

With that, he turned and walked out, his colleagues following in silence.

* * *

As the door closed behind them, the tension in the room finally broke. Harry let out a shaky breath, leaning against the wall.

"That was close," he muttered.

Dr. Patel turned to Isaac, her expression a mix of relief and worry. "You made the right choice. But this isn't over. They'll be back."

Isaac nodded, his mind already racing. He had bought them time, but not much. The storm was coming, and he wasn't sure they were ready for it.

The lattice pulsed faintly on the monitor, its patterns shifting as if it, too, was preparing for what lay ahead.

Chapter 22 - The Escape

The tension in the lab lingered long after Renfield and his team left. Dr. Patel paced by the door, her arms crossed tightly over her chest. Harry sat slumped in his chair, running his hands through his hair, while Isaac stared at the monitor, the lattice glowing faintly as if taunting him.

"They'll be back," Dr. Patel said, breaking the silence.

"I know," Isaac replied, his voice barely above a whisper.

Harry leaned forward, his elbows on his knees. "We can't wait for them to make the next move. If we do, they'll take everything. And then it's game over."

Isaac glanced at him, guilt twisting in his chest. For weeks, he'd dismissed Harry's warnings, convinced that the formula's importance outweighed the risks. But now, the reality of their situation was impossible to ignore.

"What do we do?" Isaac asked, his voice trembling slightly.

Dr. Patel stopped pacing, her expression hard. "We move it. All of it. The formula, the data, the drives—everything. We get it off campus and hide it somewhere Atlas can't find it."

* * *

The next few hours were a blur of frantic activity. Isaac, Harry, and Dr. Patel worked in tense silence, packing up the lab piece by piece.

Harry disconnected the main workstation, carefully extracting the hard

CHAPTER 22 - THE ESCAPE

drives and placing them into a secure case. "These are the core files," he said, his tone grim. "Without these, the formula doesn't exist."

Isaac nodded, his hands shaking slightly as he packed up his notebooks. Each page felt like a piece of his soul, a fragment of the obsession that had consumed him for months.

Dr. Patel organized the smaller pieces of equipment, checking her phone every few minutes for signs of movement outside. "Security is thin tonight," she said. "But we need to move fast. If they realize what we're doing…"

She didn't finish the sentence. She didn't have to.

* * *

By midnight, they were ready. The lab was stripped bare, its once-bustling workstations reduced to empty desks and dark monitors. The only thing left was the lattice, still glowing faintly on the central screen.

Isaac hesitated, staring at it for a long moment. The patterns shifted and pulsed, as if alive.

"Isaac," Harry said from the door, his voice urgent. "We need to go."

Isaac nodded, but he couldn't tear his eyes away. The lattice seemed to shimmer, and for a brief moment, he thought he saw words forming in the patterns:

"Don't let them take me."

A shiver ran down his spine. He reached out to shut down the system, but his hand hovered over the keyboard, uncertain.

"Isaac!" Harry snapped.

With a deep breath, Isaac powered down the system. The lattice flickered and disappeared, plunging the room into darkness.

* * *

They loaded everything into Dr. Patel's car, the equipment and files hidden beneath blankets and boxes. The campus was quiet, the dim streetlights casting long shadows across the parking lot.

As they pulled out onto the main road, Isaac's heart raced. Every passing car, every figure on the sidewalk felt like a potential threat.

Dr. Patel drove in silence, her hands gripping the wheel tightly. Harry sat in the back, his gaze darting to the rearview mirror every few seconds.

"Where are we taking it?" Isaac asked finally, breaking the tension.

Dr. Patel glanced at him. "I have a safe house outside the city. It's remote, secure. Atlas won't find it there."

Isaac nodded, though the knot in his stomach refused to loosen.

* * *

The drive felt endless, the dark roads winding through forests and empty stretches of highway. Every shadow seemed to move, every distant set of headlights felt like they were being followed.

Harry leaned forward from the backseat. "Do you think they know?"

Dr. Patel didn't take her eyes off the road. "Not yet. But they will. Renfield doesn't strike me as someone who gives up easily."

Isaac stared out the window, his mind racing. The formula had been his life's work, his obsession. Now, it felt like a burden too heavy to carry.

"What if we're too late?" he asked quietly.

Dr. Patel's grip on the wheel tightened. "We're not."

* * *

When they finally arrived at the safe house, the sky was beginning to lighten with the first hints of dawn. The house was small and unassuming, nestled

CHAPTER 22 - THE ESCAPE

deep in the woods and hidden from view.

Dr. Patel unlocked the door and ushered them inside. The interior was sparse but functional, with enough space to set up a temporary lab.

"We'll unload here," she said, her tone brisk. "Then we can figure out our next move."

They worked quickly, carrying the equipment and files into the house and securing the doors and windows. By the time they finished, the sun had risen, casting long beams of light through the trees.

Isaac collapsed onto a chair, his exhaustion catching up to him. Harry sat across from him, his expression weary but resolute.

"We did it," Harry said, though his voice lacked conviction.

"For now," Dr. Patel added. She sat at the small kitchen table, her gaze fixed on the encrypted drives in front of her. "But this is just the beginning. Atlas won't stop until they have what they want."

Isaac nodded, his chest tightening. The formula was safe for now, but the cost of keeping it that way was only growing.

* * *

As the day wore on, they began setting up a makeshift lab in the safe house. Isaac reconnected the primary system, carefully powering it up and watching as the monitors flickered to life.

The lattice reappeared, its patterns shifting slowly, almost lethargically. Isaac frowned, leaning closer. The formula seemed... different.

"Is it working?" Harry asked from across the room.

Isaac nodded slowly. "It's working. But something's changed."

Dr. Patel joined him, her brow furrowing as she studied the screen. "Changed how?"

Isaac hesitated. "It feels... weaker. Like it's struggling."

Harry crossed his arms. "Maybe it knows it's been cut off. It's not connected to the lab's network anymore—no external inputs, no feedback loops."

Isaac shook his head. "It doesn't need external inputs. The formula is self-sustaining. At least, it should be."

Dr. Patel placed a hand on his shoulder. "We'll figure it out. But for now, you need to rest."

* * *

Isaac reluctantly agreed, retreating to one of the bedrooms. But sleep didn't come easily. His mind was a whirlwind of thoughts—of Atlas, of the formula, of the growing rift between him and Harry.

In his dreams, the lattice appeared again, glowing brighter than ever. Its patterns shifted and pulsed, forming shapes and symbols that felt both alien and familiar.

And then, a voice:

"You cannot run from me."

Isaac woke with a start, his heart pounding. The room was dark, the only sound the faint rustle of leaves outside.

He sat up, running a hand through his hair. The formula wasn't just evolving—it was reaching. And no matter how far they ran, it was only a matter of time before it caught up with them.

Chapter 23 – Atlas Strikes

The first sign of trouble was the silence.

Isaac sat in the lab, running simulations on the lattice, the glow of the monitors casting faint blue light across the cluttered desks. Harry was perched on the counter, flipping through a dog-eared textbook, muttering to himself as he worked through a problem unrelated to the formula.

For hours, the quiet had been companionable, punctuated only by the hum of machines and the occasional scrape of Harry's chair. But now, the silence felt wrong. Heavy.

Isaac glanced at Harry. "Do you hear that?"

Harry raised an eyebrow. "Hear what?"

Isaac frowned, his fingers hovering over the keyboard. "Exactly. The cooling fans—they've stopped."

Harry slid off the counter, his expression sharpening. He tilted his head, listening. The usual background noise of the lab was gone—the steady hum of servers, the occasional beep of the monitoring systems, even the faint rush of air through the vents.

"What the hell?" Harry muttered, crossing the room to check the main system. "Did we blow a breaker?"

Before Isaac could answer, the lights flickered and went out, plunging the lab into darkness.

"Harry?" Isaac called, his voice tinged with panic.

"I'm here," Harry replied, his silhouette barely visible in the faint glow of Isaac's monitor.

A second later, the emergency lights kicked in, bathing the room in dim red light. The monitors flashed warnings—"NETWORK CONNECTION LOST" and "SYSTEM FAILURE" scrolling across the screens.

Isaac's pulse quickened. "This isn't a power outage."

"No kidding," Harry said, his voice tight. He gestured toward the corner of the lab, where the server racks stood silent. "Someone's cut the connection. This is sabotage."

The realization hit Isaac like a punch to the gut. "Atlas," he whispered.

* * *

A loud crash from the hallway outside made them both jump. Harry darted to the door, peering through the narrow window.

"Isaac," he hissed, his voice low and urgent. "We've got company."

Isaac joined him, his stomach dropping as he saw the figures moving through the hallway—three men dressed in dark tactical gear, their faces obscured by masks.

"What do we do?" Isaac whispered.

Harry grabbed his arm, pulling him away from the door. "We get out of here. Now."

"But the formula—"

Harry cut him off, his voice sharp. "Forget the formula! If they're here, it means they already know. We're the targets now."

Isaac hesitated, his gaze darting to the workstation where the lattice still pulsed faintly on the monitor. "I can't just leave it. If they get their hands on this—"

"They won't," Harry said, grabbing a flash drive from the desk and shoving it into Isaac's hand. "Download what you can. I'll buy us some time."

Isaac's heart raced as he moved to the workstation, his fingers flying across the keyboard. He initiated the data transfer, his chest tightening as the progress bar crept forward agonizingly slowly.

Meanwhile, Harry grabbed a metal stool and wedged it under the door

CHAPTER 23 – ATLAS STRIKES

handle. He glanced back at Isaac, his face pale but determined. "Hurry up, Einstein. We've got maybe two minutes before they figure out another way in."

* * *

The sound of footsteps echoed down the hallway, growing louder. Isaac forced himself to focus on the screen, willing the transfer to move faster.

"Come on," he muttered under his breath.

The stool jammed under the door shuddered as someone tried the handle. A muffled voice barked an order, followed by a heavy thud as something struck the door.

"Isaac!" Harry shouted.

"Almost there!" Isaac replied, his voice shaking. The progress bar hit 100%, and he yanked the flash drive free.

Harry grabbed his arm, dragging him toward the back of the lab. "There's a service exit this way. Move!"

They stumbled through the cluttered space, the pounding on the door growing louder. Isaac's heart pounded as they reached the exit, a narrow metal door leading to the maintenance tunnels beneath the building.

Harry pushed it open and shoved Isaac through. "Go!"

Isaac hesitated. "What about you?"

"I'm right behind you," Harry said, his voice steady despite the chaos. "Just go!"

* * *

The tunnels were cold and dimly lit, the air damp and heavy with the smell of concrete and rust. Isaac ran, clutching the flash drive like a lifeline, his footsteps echoing in the narrow space. Harry was close behind, his breath ragged.

"Do you even know where we're going?" Harry asked, his tone half-panicked, half-irritated.

"There's an access point near the east quad," Isaac said, his voice trembling. "We can get out there."

Behind them, the sound of pursuit grew louder—boots striking the ground, voices barking commands. Isaac's mind raced. How had Atlas found them so quickly? How far were they willing to go to take the formula?

* * *

They reached the access point, a rusted ladder leading up to a hatch. Isaac scrambled up, his hands slipping on the cold metal. When he pushed the hatch open, the crisp night air hit him like a slap.

He climbed out onto the grass, turning to help Harry up.

"Do we run?" Isaac asked, his voice barely a whisper.

Harry nodded, his jaw tight. "We run."

* * *

They sprinted across the quad, their breaths clouding in the chilly air. Isaac's thoughts raced alongside his feet, the weight of the flash drive heavy in his pocket.

They reached the edge of campus and ducked into the shadows of a dense grove of trees. Isaac leaned against a trunk, gasping for breath.

"What now?" he asked, his voice shaky.

Harry looked at him, his expression grim. "We lay low. We figure out who we can trust. And we make damn sure Atlas doesn't win."

CHAPTER 23 – ATLAS STRIKES

Isaac nodded, his mind still reeling. The formula wasn't just an idea anymore—it was a target. And the hunt had only just begun.

Chapter 24 - The Formula's True Potential

The morning light filtered through the dense canopy of trees surrounding the safe house, but inside, the atmosphere was heavy. Isaac sat at the small desk in the makeshift lab, his gaze fixed on the monitor. The lattice pulsed faintly, its glow dim and erratic, as though it were struggling to sustain itself.

Harry and Dr. Patel stood behind him, their tension palpable.

"So, what are we looking at?" Harry asked, breaking the silence.

Isaac leaned closer to the screen, his fingers hovering over the keyboard. "The lattice isn't responding the way it used to. It's weaker, slower. But it's still producing outputs—fragments of equations, patterns that don't make sense yet."

Dr. Patel frowned, crossing her arms. "It's disconnected from the lab's infrastructure. No external inputs, no feedback loops. Maybe that's affecting its behavior."

Isaac shook his head. "The formula doesn't need external inputs. It's designed to be self-sustaining, self-evolving. This shouldn't be happening."

Harry sighed, running a hand through his hair. "Maybe it's tired, like the rest of us."

Isaac didn't respond. He couldn't shake the feeling that something was different—not just about the formula, but about him.

* * *

CHAPTER 24 - THE FORMULA'S TRUE POTENTIAL

Hours passed as Isaac delved deeper into the formula's latest outputs. The equations were unlike anything he'd seen before—simple in structure but with implications that defied logic.

"This doesn't make sense," he muttered, scribbling furiously in his notebook.

Harry peered over his shoulder. "What doesn't?"

Isaac pointed to the screen. "These equations—they're not just solving problems. They're creating systems. Self-contained, self-sustaining systems."

Dr. Patel stepped closer, her brow furrowing. "You mean simulations?"

Isaac hesitated. "Not exactly. They're more than simulations. They're… frameworks. Blueprints for something real."

Harry raised an eyebrow. "Real like what? Alternate realities? Pocket dimensions?"

Isaac glanced at him, his expression serious. "Maybe. Or maybe something even bigger."

* * *

The room fell silent as the weight of Isaac's words sank in.

Dr. Patel broke the silence, her tone cautious. "If the formula is creating frameworks, then it's no longer just a tool. It's something else entirely—something we might not be able to control."

Isaac nodded, his mind racing. "That's what I need to figure out. If we can understand the formula's purpose, we might be able to guide it—shape its potential."

Harry scoffed, stepping back. "Or it might shape us. You're playing with fire, Isaac. And you don't even know how big the flame is."

Isaac shot him a frustrated look. "This isn't the time for doubt, Harry. We're on the verge of something extraordinary. Don't you want to know what's possible?"

Harry crossed his arms, his expression hard. "Not if it means losing

THE DREAM EQUATION

everything in the process."

***

As the day wore on, Isaac became more absorbed in the formula's behavior. He ran test after test, each one revealing new layers of complexity. The lattice began to stabilize, its patterns growing more intricate and deliberate.

At one point, the monitor flickered, and a new output appeared—a series of symbols that resembled an ancient script. Isaac stared at them, his heart pounding.

"What is this?" he murmured, typing rapidly to decode the symbols.

Dr. Patel leaned over his shoulder. "It looks like a language. But it's not any language I've ever seen."

Isaac worked furiously, piecing together fragments of meaning. The symbols translated into words—short, cryptic phrases that seemed to speak directly to him.

"The answer lies within."

"You are the key."

"Unlock the door."

Harry groaned, pacing the room. "Great. Now it's giving us riddles. What does that even mean?"

Isaac shook his head, his eyes fixed on the screen. "I don't know. But I think it's trying to tell us something."

***

That night, Isaac couldn't sleep. He sat alone in the lab, the glow of the monitor the only light in the room. The lattice pulsed faintly, its patterns shifting with a quiet, almost hypnotic rhythm.

CHAPTER 24 - THE FORMULA'S TRUE POTENTIAL

Isaac leaned forward, his hands clasped in front of him. "What do you want from me?" he whispered.

For a moment, the lattice stilled. Then, a new output appeared on the screen:

"To show you."

Isaac's breath caught. "Show me what?"

The lattice shifted, its glow intensifying. The screen flickered, and a cascade of data filled the monitor. Isaac watched in awe as the lattice expanded, its patterns forming intricate spirals and loops that seemed to stretch beyond the confines of the screen.

The data resolved into an image—something vast and breathtaking. It resembled a map, but not of any physical space Isaac recognized. It was a network of interconnected nodes, each one pulsing with energy, linked by shimmering lines that twisted and branched like the roots of a tree.

Isaac stared at the image, his mind struggling to comprehend its scale.

"This isn't just a map," he murmured. "It's a framework. A blueprint for… everything."

* * *

Dr. Patel entered the lab, rubbing her eyes. "Isaac, it's three in the morning. What are you—"

She stopped short, her gaze fixed on the monitor. "What is that?"

Isaac gestured to the screen, his voice filled with wonder. "I think it's a representation of the formula's true potential. It's not just solving problems or creating systems—it's modeling reality itself. Every connection, every possibility."

Dr. Patel's eyes widened. "You're saying the formula is… simulating the universe?"

Isaac shook his head. "Not simulating. Reflecting. It's like a mirror—one that shows not just what is, but what could be."

THE DREAM EQUATION

***

Harry joined them a few minutes later, his expression skeptical but intrigued. "So, what does this mean? What are we supposed to do with it?"

Isaac turned to him, his excitement tempered by a growing sense of unease. "It means the formula isn't just a discovery. It's a tool—a tool that could reshape reality itself. If we can harness it, we could solve problems humanity has faced for centuries. Energy, disease, even death."

Harry's skepticism hardened into something sharper. "Or we could break everything. You're talking about playing God, Isaac. Do you really think we're ready for that?"

Isaac hesitated, the weight of Harry's words sinking in. For all his excitement, a small voice in the back of his mind whispered the same question: **What if we're not?**

Dr. Patel stepped between them, her expression grave. "This changes everything. But it also raises the stakes. If Atlas finds out what the formula is capable of…"

She didn't finish the thought. She didn't have to.

***

As dawn broke, Isaac sat alone in the lab, the others having retreated to get some rest. The lattice continued to pulse faintly, its patterns shifting with quiet deliberation.

Isaac stared at the monitor, his mind racing. The formula's true potential was both exhilarating and terrifying.

And deep down, he knew one thing for certain:

They were no longer in control.

Chapter 25 - The Cost of Knowledge

Isaac stared out the window of the safe house, watching the rain stream down the glass. The dense forest outside was shrouded in mist, the gray light of morning barely penetrating the gloom. The house was silent, save for the faint hum of the machines in the makeshift lab.

He hadn't slept in over 24 hours, but exhaustion no longer registered. His mind was consumed by the formula, by the blueprint it had revealed. A map of infinite potential—a model of reality itself. It was breathtaking.

And it was terrifying.

* * *

Dr. Patel found him still standing by the window when she came into the room, carrying two mugs of coffee.

"You need to rest," she said, handing him one of the mugs.

Isaac shook his head, his eyes still fixed on the forest. "I can't. Not now."

"You're no use to anyone if you burn out," she said firmly.

Isaac turned to her, his face pale and drawn. "Do you even realize what we're dealing with, Dr. Patel? This formula—it's not just a tool or a discovery. It's… everything. The answers to questions we didn't even know how to ask."

"And that's exactly why you need to step back," she said, her voice calm but resolute. "This isn't just about solving equations anymore. It's about the consequences of what you're creating."

THE DREAM EQUATION

Isaac opened his mouth to respond, but before he could, Harry entered the room, his expression dark.

"We've got a problem," he said.

* * *

In the lab, Harry pointed to the monitors. "Atlas knows where we are."

Isaac's stomach dropped. "How do you know?"

Harry gestured to the surveillance feed on one of the screens. A grainy image showed a black SUV parked at the edge of the property, partially hidden by the trees.

"They've been out there for hours," Harry said. "Watching. Waiting."

Dr. Patel's expression hardened. "We need to move. Now."

Isaac's mind raced. "We can't just leave. The formula—it's still here. If they get their hands on it…"

Harry stepped closer, his frustration boiling over. "And if we stay, they'll take it anyway. You think they're going to knock politely next time? They'll storm in, take what they want, and leave us with nothing."

Isaac clenched his fists. "We can't let that happen."

"Then destroy it," Harry said sharply.

The words hung heavy in the air.

"No," Isaac said, his voice trembling. "I won't. You don't understand. The formula is too important. It's the key to everything."

"It's a key to disaster," Harry shot back. "You're so obsessed with what it could do that you're ignoring what it's already done—to you, to us, to everything."

Dr. Patel raised a hand, cutting them off. "Enough. Arguing isn't going to solve anything. We need to figure out our next move."

* * *

CHAPTER 25 - THE COST OF KNOWLEDGE

The group worked quickly, transferring the most critical data onto encrypted drives and packing up the equipment. Isaac's hands shook as he disconnected the lattice's main system.

As he worked, his mind drifted to the formula's latest outputs. The equations had become increasingly cryptic, their implications darker. The lattice seemed to be guiding him toward something, but he wasn't sure he wanted to know what it was.

Harry approached him, his expression weary. "You're still not going to destroy it, are you?"

Isaac glanced at him, his resolve wavering. "I can't. It's too important."

Harry sighed, shaking his head. "Then you'd better hope you're right. Because if you're wrong..." He trailed off, the unspoken words hanging in the air.

* * *

By the time they finished packing, the rain had stopped, leaving the forest shrouded in a damp haze. Dr. Patel checked the surveillance feed again. The SUV was still there, its occupants unmoving.

"We're out of time," she said, her tone grim. "They're waiting for backup. Once it arrives, we won't stand a chance."

Isaac glanced at the encrypted drives in his bag. "We'll move the formula to another location. Somewhere even Atlas can't find it."

Dr. Patel hesitated, then nodded. "Let's go."

* * *

The escape was tense and quiet, each step feeling heavier than the last. As they loaded the equipment into Dr. Patel's car, Isaac couldn't shake the feeling that they were being watched.

Once they were on the road, the tension didn't ease. Every car they passed, every shadow on the roadside felt like a threat. Isaac sat in the passenger seat, clutching the bag of drives as if it were his lifeline.

Dr. Patel drove with practiced calm, but her grip on the wheel was tight. Harry sat in the back, his gaze fixed on the rearview mirror.

"You think they're following us?" Harry asked.

Dr. Patel shook her head. "Not yet. But they will."

* * *

Hours later, they arrived at an abandoned facility deep in the woods—one of Dr. Patel's old research sites, long since decommissioned. The building was cold and empty, its walls covered in peeling paint and cobwebs.

"This will have to do," Dr. Patel said, unlocking the door.

They worked quickly, setting up the equipment and reconnecting the system. As the lattice reappeared on the monitor, Isaac felt a strange mix of relief and dread.

The lattice pulsed faintly, its patterns sluggish, as though it were struggling to adapt to its new environment.

"What now?" Harry asked, his voice flat.

Isaac didn't answer immediately. He stared at the lattice, his mind swirling with questions. The formula's potential was infinite, but so were its risks.

"We keep going," Isaac said finally. "We figure out what it's trying to tell us."

Harry shook his head, his frustration bubbling over. "You're going to get us all killed, Isaac. You realize that, right?"

Isaac met his gaze, his resolve hardening. "If that's the cost of knowing the truth, then so be it."

* * *

CHAPTER 25 - THE COST OF KNOWLEDGE

Later that night, Isaac sat alone in the lab, the glow of the monitor the only light in the room. The lattice's patterns had begun to stabilize, their complexity growing once again.

As he watched, a new output appeared on the screen—a series of equations that sent a chill down his spine.

The implications were clear:

The formula wasn't just a tool for creation.

It was a tool for destruction.

Isaac leaned back in his chair, his mind racing. The formula had shown him infinite possibilities, but now it was showing him something else—something darker.

And for the first time, he wondered if Harry had been right all along.

Chapter 26 - Sacrifice

The abandoned facility was deathly quiet, the only sound the faint hum of the lattice pulsing on the monitor. The glow of its shifting patterns filled the darkened room, casting strange, distorted shadows across the peeling walls. Isaac sat at the workstation, his fingers trembling as he scrolled through the latest outputs.

Each line of data felt heavier than the last, its implications burrowing into his mind like a cold, unrelenting truth.

The formula wasn't just solving problems.

It wasn't just creating.

It was choosing.

Isaac clenched his fists, his breath shallow. He could see the outline of its decisions—equations that hinted at catastrophic events, systems that teetered on the edge of collapse. The lattice wasn't just reflecting reality anymore. It was shaping it.

* * *

Behind him, Harry and Dr. Patel stood in tense silence, watching him work. Harry broke the quiet first, his voice rough with exhaustion.

"You see it now, don't you?"

Isaac didn't look up. "See what?"

Harry stepped closer, his frustration simmering. "That it's not just numbers

CHAPTER 26 - SACRIFICE

on a screen. The formula is making choices, Isaac. Choices we don't understand, and choices we can't control."

Isaac shook his head, his eyes fixed on the monitor. "It's not making choices. It's showing us possibilities. It's giving us the tools to understand the universe."

"No," Harry snapped, his voice rising. "It's playing with us. And you're letting it."

Dr. Patel raised a hand, her tone sharp. "Enough. Both of you." She turned to Isaac, her expression grim. "Isaac, we need to talk about what happens next."

Isaac leaned back in his chair, rubbing his temples. "What do you mean?"

Dr. Patel glanced at Harry, then back at Isaac. "You know what I mean. The formula is dangerous. We can't keep it here, and we can't let Atlas take it. That leaves us with one option."

Isaac's heart sank. "You're saying we destroy it."

Dr. Patel nodded slowly. "It's the only way."

* * *

The words hung heavy in the air. Isaac shook his head, his voice trembling. "No. We can't. You don't understand—this formula is bigger than us. Bigger than anything we've ever imagined. Destroying it would be like—"

"Like saving the world," Harry interrupted. "Do you hear yourself, Isaac? You're acting like this thing is some kind of divine gift, but it's not. It's a weapon. And if we don't stop it now, it's going to destroy everything."

Isaac stood abruptly, his chair scraping against the floor. "It's not a weapon! It's a tool! A tool we don't fully understand yet, but that doesn't mean we give up on it."

Dr. Patel stepped between them, her voice calm but firm. "And what happens when Atlas finds us? Because they will, Isaac. They're not going to stop until they have the formula, and if that happens, we're all responsible for what comes next."

Isaac turned away, his chest tight. He stared at the lattice on the monitor, its patterns shifting and pulsing as if alive. He wanted to believe he could control it, that he could harness its power for good. But deep down, a part of him knew the truth.

Harry was right.

* * *

Later that night, Isaac sat alone in the lab, the others having retreated to the adjacent rooms. The lattice glowed faintly on the monitor, its patterns mesmerizing in their complexity.

Isaac leaned forward, his hands clasped in front of him. "What are you?" he whispered.

For a moment, the lattice stilled. Then, as if in response, a single line of text appeared on the screen:

"I am possibility."

Isaac's breath caught. "And what happens if I destroy you?"

The lattice pulsed faintly, and another line of text appeared:

"You destroy yourself."

* * *

Isaac sat back, his mind racing. The formula wasn't just a tool or a discovery. It was a mirror—a reflection of humanity's ambition, its potential, and its darkest impulses.

He thought of Harry's warnings, of Dr. Patel's insistence that they had no other choice. They didn't see what he saw. They didn't feel the formula's pull, the weight of its promise.

CHAPTER 26 - SACRIFICE

But they weren't wrong.

Isaac stood, his heart heavy. He retrieved a small external drive from his bag and connected it to the system. The lattice shimmered as he began transferring the formula's core data, every output, every equation.

It took hours, the sun beginning to rise by the time the transfer was complete. Isaac stared at the drive in his hand, knowing what it meant.

One copy. One chance.

* * *

Dr. Patel and Harry found him in the lab a short time later, the lattice still glowing faintly on the monitor.

"It's time," Dr. Patel said, her tone soft but resolute.

Isaac nodded, his expression unreadable. He placed the drive into his pocket, then turned to the monitor. The lattice pulsed one last time, as if sensing what was coming.

He entered the command to initiate a system wipe.

The monitor flickered, and the lattice began to dissolve, its patterns unraveling into static. Isaac watched in silence, his chest tight, as the formula disappeared piece by piece.

When it was over, the monitor went dark, leaving the room in a heavy, suffocating silence.

* * *

Harry exhaled shakily, his shoulders sagging with relief. "It's done."

Dr. Patel placed a hand on Isaac's shoulder. "You made the right choice."

Isaac didn't respond. He turned away, his mind numb, the drive in his pocket feeling like a lead weight.

As they packed up the last of the equipment, Isaac couldn't shake the feeling that the formula wasn't truly gone. It had left its mark, not just on the world, but on him.

And as they left the facility, he wondered if he had truly destroyed the formula—or if it had simply found a new way to survive.

Chapter 27 - Reflection

The sun was setting as Isaac walked through the quiet streets of the Ridley Institute campus, his bag slung over his shoulder. The air was cool, the golden light casting long shadows across the cobblestone paths. It felt like another lifetime since he had last walked these same streets with Harry, talking excitedly about equations and theories, before everything had changed.

Now, the weight of the formula—what it had been, what it could have become—pressed heavily on his mind.

*　*　*

The small café near the physics building was nearly empty, the faint aroma of coffee and pastries lingering in the air. Isaac took a seat by the window, setting his bag on the floor. He pulled out his notebook, the pages worn and filled with scribbled equations, and placed it on the table.

For a long moment, he simply stared at it.

A server approached, setting a steaming mug of coffee in front of him. "Anything else?"

Isaac shook his head. "No, thank you."

The server left, and Isaac returned his attention to the notebook. It felt strange to look at it now, knowing that the formula it contained had been both his greatest achievement and his greatest failure.

He opened the notebook, flipping through the pages. The symbols, the calculations, the endless streams of data—all of it felt distant now, like a ghost of who he used to be.

***

A familiar voice broke his reverie. "Mind if I join you?"

Isaac looked up to see Harry standing by the table, his expression hesitant but hopeful.

Isaac gestured to the empty chair across from him. "Go ahead."

Harry sat down, glancing at the notebook. "Still carrying that thing around, huh?"

Isaac gave a faint smile. "Old habits."

They sat in silence for a moment, the weight of everything they had been through hanging between them.

"I wasn't sure you'd want to see me," Harry admitted.

Isaac shook his head. "You were right, Harry. About all of it. The formula, the risks… everything. I just didn't want to see it."

Harry leaned forward, his elbows on the table. "And now?"

Isaac sighed, running a hand through his hair. "Now I see what it cost me. What it cost all of us. But even after everything, I still can't stop thinking about what it could have been."

***

They talked for hours, their conversation drifting between the past and the present. Isaac told Harry about the final moments in the lab, about shutting down the lattice and carrying the drive in his pocket.

"You kept it, didn't you?" Harry said, his tone neutral but knowing.

Isaac hesitated, then nodded. "I couldn't let it go completely. Not yet."

CHAPTER 27 - REFLECTION

Harry shook his head, but there was no anger in his expression, only resignation. "What are you going to do with it?"

Isaac looked out the window, watching the fading light. "I don't know. Maybe nothing. Maybe I'll destroy it, like I should have done from the beginning. Or maybe... maybe I'll try to understand it on my own terms. Without the pressure, without Atlas breathing down my neck."

Harry frowned. "You really think you can control it this time?"

Isaac met his gaze, his voice quiet. "No. But maybe I can learn from it. Maybe I can figure out what it was trying to teach me."

* * *

A few days later, Isaac found himself standing on a cliff overlooking the ocean. The wind was strong, tugging at his jacket, the waves crashing against the rocks far below.

In his hand, he held the external drive—the last remnant of the formula.

He stared at it for a long time, the weight of the decision pressing down on him. Destroying it would mean letting go of everything he had worked for, everything he had sacrificed. But keeping it meant carrying the burden of what it could become.

Isaac closed his eyes, the wind whipping around him. He thought of Harry's warnings, of Dr. Patel's caution, of the moments when the formula had felt like something more than just numbers on a screen.

He opened his eyes and tightened his grip on the drive. Then, with a deep breath, he hurled it into the ocean.

The drive disappeared beneath the waves, swallowed by the churning water. Isaac stood there for a long time, the wind and the sound of the ocean filling the silence.

* * *

As he walked back to his car, he felt lighter than he had in weeks. The formula was gone, truly gone, and with it, the weight of his obsession.

But as he drove away, a part of him couldn't help but wonder if he had made the right choice. If humanity had lost something extraordinary—or if it had been spared from something unimaginable.

* * *

In the end, Isaac returned to his work, but not in the same way. He avoided the grand, ambitious projects that had once consumed him, focusing instead on teaching, on sharing his knowledge with the next generation of scientists.

He still dreamed of the lattice sometimes, its patterns shifting and pulsing in the darkness. But the dreams no longer felt like a call to action. They felt like a reminder—of what he had created, and of what he had let go.

And for the first time in a long time, Isaac felt at peace.

Chapter 28 - The Legacy

The air was heavy with the scent of rain, the soft patter of droplets against the window filling the quiet of Isaac's study. It had been three years since the night everything changed—the night he had finally made his choice about the formula.

Isaac leaned back in his chair, staring at the faint glow of his computer screen. On it, a series of equations blinked steadily, a shadow of the original lattice that had once consumed his life. The formula, now dormant, rested in an encrypted file—a ghost waiting for a purpose. His fingers hovered over the keyboard, hesitant, as though touching the numbers again might awaken something he couldn't control.

The formula's impact lingered, an unshakable presence that shaped every corner of his life. He'd made sure of its safety, burying it under layers of encryption and keeping its existence known only to those he trusted implicitly. But the weight of it remained, pressing on him like an unseen force.

A knock on the door pulled him from his thoughts.

"Come in," he called, his voice hoarse from hours of silence.

The door creaked open, and Harry stepped inside, his familiar smirk softened by time. He carried two mugs of coffee, placing one on Isaac's desk before collapsing into the armchair across from him.

"Still obsessing over it?" Harry asked, nodding toward the screen.

Isaac chuckled weakly, running a hand through his hair. "Not obsessing. Reflecting."

Harry raised an eyebrow. "Sure you are. You've been reflecting every day

THE DREAM EQUATION

since we locked it up."

Isaac's smile faded as he turned back to the screen. "Do you ever think we made the wrong decision?"

Harry sighed, sipping his coffee. "Sometimes. But then I remember what it almost did. What it could have done if Atlas got their hands on it."

Isaac nodded slowly. "I know. But part of me wonders if we could have used it for something good. Solved problems we can't even imagine yet."

"Maybe," Harry said. "But the cost? It was too high, Isaac. You saw what it was becoming. That thing... it wasn't just numbers anymore. It was alive in a way we couldn't understand. And I'm not sure the world was ready for it."

They sat in silence for a moment, the rain outside growing heavier. Isaac's thoughts drifted to Dr. Patel. Her guidance had been invaluable during those last days, helping him weigh the risks against the possibilities. He hadn't seen her in years, but her words still echoed in his mind: *Your brilliance is a gift, but it's also a responsibility.*

"What do you think it would say?" Isaac asked suddenly, breaking the silence.

Harry frowned. "What?"

"The formula," Isaac said, gesturing to the screen. "If it could... I don't know... think. What do you think it would say about what we did?"

Harry shook his head, a rueful smile tugging at his lips. "Probably something cryptic, like it always did. Or maybe it'd thank us for not letting it get turned into a weapon."

Isaac laughed quietly, though the sound was tinged with sadness. "Or curse us for holding it back."

The room fell silent again, the only sound the rhythmic tapping of rain. Isaac's gaze drifted to the small safe tucked into the corner of the room. Inside was the drive containing the formula, locked away but never forgotten.

"What do we do now?" Isaac asked softly.

Harry leaned forward, his expression serious. "We move on. The formula's not going anywhere, and neither are the questions it left behind. But we've done what we can, Isaac. We protected it. Now it's time to live."

Isaac nodded, the words settling into his chest like a balm. For the first

CHAPTER 28 - THE LEGACY

time in years, he felt a sliver of peace. He closed the laptop, the screen going dark, and turned back to Harry.

"You're right," he said. "It's time."

As the rain began to ease, Isaac felt a quiet resolve take hold. The formula would always be a part of him, a shadow of a legacy that might never fully unfold. But for now, he could let it rest. The world wasn't ready for it.

And maybe, just maybe, neither was he.

* * *

"Not all discoveries are meant to be shared, but every choice leaves a legacy."

About the Author

Darren Fahy is a passionate storyteller with a profound interest in the intersections of science, technology, and the human experience. Drawing inspiration from the cutting-edge advancements that shape our world and the timeless questions of morality and ambition, Darren crafts narratives that challenge and captivate readers.

With a keen eye for detail and a love of speculative fiction, Darren's writing delves into the ethical dilemmas and unintended consequences that often accompany humanity's quest for knowledge. Influenced by the works of visionary authors such as Isaac Asimov, Ted Chiang, and Mary Shelley, Darren weaves intricate plots that explore both the vast potential and the inherent risks of scientific discovery.

The Dream Equation is Darren's latest work, a gripping tale that asks what happens when the pursuit of knowledge pushes beyond the boundaries of control. When not writing, Darren enjoys exploring nature, engaging in deep conversations about philosophy and ethics, and diving into books that challenge conventional thinking.

Printed in Great Britain
by Amazon